VERA

For Sherrie and the girls.

2

Printed in the United States of America

Prologue

Vera heard the car coming before she saw it.
The headlights crested the hill at the end of
the street and the engine knocked with the
stress he had put on it for the nearly thirty
miles he would have to travel to get here.
She knew he would be coming and that he
would be pissed. He would be violent. He

had likely been drinking since he got out of work at five, which gave him six hours to get absolutely loaded.

The lawyer said that the papers would be served today, that she should go stay with family until his initial anger wore off. It wouldn't. Her sister, Brenda, insisted that she come stay with her for the weekend while Craig packed his things and got out of the house. She didn't want to feel like a burden on her family- they assured her she would never be a burden- and she relented.

She waited anxiously for any sign that Craig had been served the divorce papers, pacing anxiously as the kids played in the fresh snow. Eventually she joined in with them and, for a moment, forgot about the anxiety that ate away at her since she filed the paperwork.

The phone calls started three hours before and hadn't ceased. As soon as one call ended, another would come. The times he did leave voicemails sent shivers up her spine.

"If I can't have you, nobody is going to. I'm going to fucking kill you." He said, "Somebody is going to get hurt tonight and it's not going to be me, bitch."

The last straw was the prostitutes. She knew he hadn't been faithful for a long time, but when he was arrested for luring prostitutes into his work truck with crack cocaine, that was the line in the sand. She filed the divorce paperwork the Monday following his arrest.

The car's exhaust billowed in the cold winter air. It snowed most of the day, several inches covering the roadway as the tail end of the '98 Skylark swung dangerously out of control.

"Oh, fuck he's here!" Vera screamed. Her sister had already woken her niece and nephew, prepared to escape out the back door should he make his way into the house. Paul, her brother-in-law stood waiting, twelve gauge shotgun in hand.

"If he comes in here he's a dead man." He said angrily.

The Skylark roared up the road at a reckless speed. He cut the wheel too sharply and missed his turn, skidding through her sister's snow-covered yard. The front end slammed into the dirty pile of snow and ice they shoveled from the driveway earlier in the day, and the front end of the car went airborne, headlights shining into the sky and illuminating the still falling snow. They looked like tiny white dancers fluttering silently in the night. The car rested atop the pile of snow like an adventurer reaching the summit of Everest.

"Paul, he's getting out of the car!" Brenda said, hurrying the kids toward the kitchen and to the back door, still trying to get them to get their winter boots on. The kids argued about leaving their dad and Vera, but a few light whacks from Brenda got them going the right speed.

"WHERE THE FUCK ARE YOU VERA!"   She heard his slurred speech and his shambling lanky silhouette shambled up the icy driveway, he looked like a zombie from an old Romero movie, the ones she used to stay up late watching with her dad.

"Brenda, get the kids out of here!" hissed Paul, racking a shell into the chamber of the shotgun.

"Don't," Vera said, placing her hand calmly on the gun, "Don't shoot him."

"If he comes in here I'm cutting him in half with it," said Paul bluntly, "I mean it, Vera."

She stepped outside, "Go home, Craig. It's over."

"Fuck you!" he shrieked. The neighbor's houses began to light up.

"I called the police, Craig! Get out of here!" yelled Brenda from the doorway. She returned for her own boots, having forgotten them in the fray.

"I'll fucking kill you, Brenda!" Craig yelled, finger jabbing with each word.

"The fuck you will!" yelled Paul, stepping into Craig's view for the first time and raising the shotgun, the barrel leveled at the drunken man's chest, "I'll empty this damn thing, Craig. Leave."

"Tough man with a gun!" laughed Craig in a sing-song, "Put that thing down and let's see how tough you are."

Paul outweighed Craig by nearly seventy pounds. It wasn't all muscle, but most of it was. Craig was wiry and always looked stretched too thin now.. The alcohol fueled his confidence to his detriment.

"Hey! Some of us are trying to sleep!" yelled one elderly neighbor from the safety of his screen door.

"I'll kill you next, old man!" Craig hollered, his fist raised in the general direction the voice had come from.

"Craig," said Vera, "You aren't killing anyone."

He made it to the front porch of her sister's house by now, struggling to keep his balance on the slight incline which led to it.

She stood before him, arms crossed. She wasn't going to give in this time.

"Come with me. Now." he said, his voice filled with dead hate and spoken through gritted teeth.

"No." she said matter-of-factly, "You need to leave. It's over. I'm not putting up with this anymore!"

"I'm giving you one more chance, Vera. Get the fucking keys to your truck and get in." again with that same cold voice. He shook with rage. His eyes were bloodshot and she could smell the sour whiskey and beer on his breath.

She pulled the keys from her coat pocket, throwing them at his feet. They stuck in the snow like daggers.

"Take your damn truck. I don't want it."

It was true, she hated that damn truck. A massive Ford F250 that guzzled gas and garnered stares from passer-bys due to the obnoxious lift kit and exhaust he had installed on it.

"You think I'm just going to let you leave, huh?" he chortled, "Is that it?"

"You don't have to *let* me do anything. I *will* do whatever I want, and I *want* a divorce."

He struck her with a speed that she would have thought impossible in his inebriated state, grasping at the collar of her shirt and tearing it down the front as he did, exposing her bra. Vera saw stars and felt a trickle of blood from her nose, spilling over her lip.

He hadn't broken it but damage had been done. He hit her twice more in the face, each blow rattling her closer to unconsciousness.

Paul raised the shotgun but couldn't fire it without risking hitting Vera. He tossed it inside and dove from the porch, tackling the both of them into the snow, his 250 lb frame slamming into them at full force. Unfortunately, Vera took the brunt of that blow, the wind had been knocked clear out of her and she gulped like a fish out of water.

In the distance Vera could hear her nephew and niece screaming for the neighbors to let them in, their frantic cries stabbing at her heart. She brought this mess to their doorstep. She could hear glass shattering and the screams were joined by yells of confusion. She wondered what the hell was going on over there.

  She made it to her knees, only to be kicked in the stomach by Craig, who made it to his feet first. Paul was behind him, yanking at his waist trying to keep him from reaching Vera. Vera gasped dryly, but no air would enter her lungs. For several seconds she thought she might be dying, that he had ruptured her lungs and she would die in the snow covered yard, but eventually she sucked in air as tears streamed from her face.

  Air!

  Paul lifted Craig into the air, throwing his weight backwards, and slammed him head first into the snow. He scurried free of Paul's grasp as if unaffected and darted quickly at Vera, throwing his arm around her throat, pulling her to her feet, and holding her between Paul and himself.

"Stay back! I'll break her goddamn neck!" he hissed. He sounded like a venomous snake in her ear and she shivered at the sound. He squeezed tighter and she choked, gagging at the pressure he was applying. Her arms clawed helplessly at his arm.

"Let her go!" Paul yelled.

"Toss me the keys, now!" said Craig, gesturing at them with his head. They still lay where Vera had tossed them, plunged into the snow like some mythical sword in the stone.

Vera could see the blood in the snow. Her blood. It looked black in the snowy dark. She knew that she was going to die tonight.

Vera nodded at Paul frantically, trying to will him to give Craig the keys, if only so he would relax the grip that he had around her throat and allow her to breathe. Her vision began to darken as Craig squeezed tighter yet, just to prove his point.

"Okay, okay!" surrendered Paul, hands up in surrender as he retrieved the keys.

"Give them to her," he demanded.
Paul edged forward slowly, keeping his hands raised in surrender. Vera saw the fear in his face. He carefully placed the keys in Vera's outstretched hand. She handed them

off to Craig, who relieved some of the pressure. She gasped in sharp breaths that burned at her throat and lungs like breathing smoke.

He dragged her toward the Ford. Paul followed but she showed him her palm, telling him to stop. She had never seen Craig like this before. It had gotten bad many times, but this was a whole new level, even for him.

"You cowardly prick." Paul said, fist balled in anger staring after them. She could see every bit of him wanting to tear her husband into bloody pieces.

Craig only smiled at him as he forced Vera into the truck through the driver side door, shoving her hard. Her head connected with the passenger window, violently rocking her head. He climbed in behind her and fired up the truck.

It was then that he pulled the pistol from the back of his pants. He somehow had managed to keep it during the scuffle and now pointed it at her, "Sit there and shut up."

He threw the truck into reverse, hurling rocks and ice at the underside of the truck in loud bangs and clanks. Several struck the house punching holes into the vinyl siding with loud cracking blows. He hurled it into drive, the transmission lurching violently and the truck slammed forward.

He sped through the yard, the truck rattling violently across uneven snowy terrain. He hit the stop sign, which sat like an exclamation point near the garden and the road. The sign showered sparks in the night as it was thrown across the concrete. It would have gone through the neighbor's picture window had it not embedded itself in the tall flower box in their yard, sending chunks of wood and plastic flying.

Craig slammed the brakes, throwing Vera into the dash, laughing as he did. The truck came to a stop broadside of the house.

Paul still stood in the yard, watching the chaos in shock. She heard the electronic whirring of the driver side window and saw Craig raise the pistol and aim it.

"You're dead you fat fuck!" he cackled maniacally. He was completely insane with rage. Vera's head ached in dull throbs, like a slow poison taking effect.

Paul threw himself to the ground and tried to stay low as he looked for cover, crawling toward the house. Craig pulled the trigger three times. He turned to Vera, bloodshot eyes wide with excitement,"Told you I was going to kill him."

She couldn't tell if Paul had been hit by the gunfire or if Craig was bluffing. Her ears rang violently from the gunshots and her vision reminded her of those waving sequences that old movies used to do when someone was coming out of a dream. Craig was occupied with yelling more obscenities out of the window. She hated that she could

smell his body odor. Vera saw her
opportunity.

She yanked the door open and rolled out,
kicking the door shut behind her as she did.
She hit the concrete hard, it felt like cold
knives on her hands, but she forced herself
to keep moving. He was going to kill her, or
worse yet, everyone he could.

She heard muffled yelling as Craig fired
two shots through the door, missing her
wildly, but still too close for comfort. She
skittered around the tailgate and up into the
yard. The high whine of the truck's engine
roared again and her shadow suddenly
appeared in front of her. The headlights
swung past her as he reversed, and then
focused on her once again, her shadow

jumping out in front of her like a shambling corpse. Craig laid into the accelerator and charged toward her through the cold winter night.

"He's going to run me over!" she thought. It would have been the last thought that went through her mind had Paul not snatched her from where he had been hiding behind the large maple tree which stood near the porch. The truck swerved to miss the house and slammed into the Skylark that Craig had buried in the snowbank.

"We gotta run!" he said, yanking at her. The white reverse lights blinked on..

They took off around the opposite side of the house- putting it between Craig and them- taking the narrow path that ran between Paul and Brenda's house and the empty house that sat next door.

Craig reversed the truck until he had a clear view of the path and opened fire. Vera heard the bullets as they passed, a high whine electrifying the air above their heads. She let out a scream as she slipped on the downslope of the yard and fell to her knees. Paul pulled her along until she regained her footing. The gunshots turned into clicks, she could hear them over the idling engine. He was out of ammo, for now at least. The engine roared again and the truck shot out of sight.

The snow slowed their progress as they frantically made for the neighbor's house. Sirens blared several miles away and were slowly growing closer. Help was coming, but at this rate she wasn't sure they would make it in time.

She saw headlights appear through the holes in the fencing along the side of the backyard that hugged the street, creating long shadows that reached out for them like spidery fingers. She only had a moment to register what was going to happen before it did.

The enormous red truck exploded through the fence like a wild animal escaping captivity, bucking violently through the embankment that the snowplow had created alongside the road. The fence splintered as if hit by dynamite, scattering across the fresh powder in dark jagged pieces. The truck

gave one last loud clunk and stalled,
skidding to an awkward stop in the middle
of the yard. Smoke poured from under the
hood.

Vera and Paul stood staring in awe as Craig
opened the door of the cab and slipped out
onto one of the cold, hard-packed trails that
the kids had already worn into the snow. He
cradled his arm as if it were a swaddled
baby and he was crying.

"VERA! VERA, YOU BITCH!" he
screamed from his back. He didn't attempt
to rise, only kicked like a toddler who hadn't
gotten his way.

"Come on." Paul said, leading the way
over the small fence between his yard and
the neighbors. They found a pile of glass

where the neighbors sliding glass door had been on the side of the house.

"Hello?" Paul called out, "It's Paul and Vera."

Vera saw a short plump woman with gray hair appear, wide eyed, "You kids get upstairs! Brenda and the kids are already up there. We called the cops."

"So did Brenda, they need to hurry the hell up!" Paul said, "Where are they when you really need them?"

As if on cue, Vera saw the blue and red lights reflecting off of the trees down the street and watched as two police cruisers slid around the corner one after the other.

Craig was trying to start the truck. It would crank loudly, grind, backfire and then stall. "Got you now, you fuck." Vera thought to herself.

They climbed the stairs quickly and found Brenda and the kids, glued to the window watching the scene unfold in their backyard below. Dustin, Vera's nephew, a decent sized red stain spread across the back of his shirt.

"What happened?" Vera asked worriedly, fearing he had been hit by one of the stray bullets.

Dustin, who she still considered a kid although he was quickly becoming a young adult at sixteen, shrugged it off, "They couldn't hear us pounding on the door to let us in. So I broke the window and a piece of the glass stabbed me in the shoulder. I think I'm okay, though."

Vera heard the policemen yelling at Craig through the window that Brenda had pushed open.

"Get on the ground, now! Don't move!"

Craig stood defiantly in the snow below. Three police officers with guns raised had him cornered. There was no escape this time. She could almost see the petulant child-like rage that had been fueling his rampage boil off of him.

"GO FUCK YOURSELVES, PIGS! SOMEBODY IS GETTING HURT TONIGHT AND IT'S NOT GONNA BE-" Craig had begun but was cut short.

He hadn't seen the fourth officer that quietly circled the house with his stun gun in hand. He raised it and shot Craig square in the back. He went rigid, falling face first into the snow with a loud THUD!. His body twitched as the electricity coursed through him. Vera felt a guilty happiness at this, and smiled slightly when the kids snickered even through the shock at what had just transpired.

They cuffed him and none too gently, making sure that his head bounced off the frame of the cruiser as they helped him into it.

Vera heard the change in Craig's tone, telling the cops that his whore wife had been cheating on him and that he had only done what any man would do in his situation, they had to believe him. He sounded as though he were crying.

That was Craig, always the victim. They silenced him by slamming the door on him mid-sentence.

Vera sat back on the floor in relief, taking in her injuries. Bloody nose, scuffed knee, probably a couple of bruised- if not broken- ribs, definitely a concussion from where she had hit her head on the window. She only now realized that her shirt was torn and pulled the tattered remains together modestly, embarrassed at being revealed in such a way.

"Here, dear," said the older woman who had greeted them at the shattered door, "Put this on." She handed Vera an old Carhart. Vera thanked her and put it on, she hadn't realized how cold she had been.

"No need to thank me. Any family of Paul and Brenda's is family of ours. Last year he woke us up in the night when Brenda saw we had a chimney fire, came running over in his underwear and everything. Would have burned alive if not for them." said the old woman smiling, "I'm Susie."

The introduction was interrupted by the sound of glass on concrete and Vera saw that Craig had kicked out the cruiser window and was sliding out of it. He landed shoulder first on the blacktop as he dropped from the cruiser. Even from this distance Vera felt the audible pop as the shoulder was dislocated. Craig's screams once again filled the night, this time instead of rage they were full of pain as they tased him and tossed him in the back of the other cruiser, once again banging his head off of the door frame.

"Jesus" said Brenda, her hand covering her mouth involuntarily "I can't believe that just happened."

"I can't either," said Vera truthfully, "I knew it was going to be bad, but I didn't know it was going to be *this* bad."

She couldn't have known that it was going to be this bad. In the five years that they had been married, and the ten years they had been together, he had never done anything this severe. Sure, there had been times when he lost his temper, but never with the homicidal fury that had overtaken him tonight.

"Vera!" Paul yelled up the stairs, "The police are down here and they need a statement!"

"Do you want me to come with you?" Brenda asked, wiping tears from her eyes. The reality of the situation had hit her and she had begun to cry.

"I think I'll be okay," Vera said, grimacing as she rose to her feet. She would have to get her ribs looked at by the doctor tomorrow, they were already aching.

By the time Vera finished giving her statement the adrenaline had worn off and she felt the aches and pains more acutely.

She was pleased to see Craig weeping in the backseat of the cruiser as it pulled away. He had just made the divorce much easier for her, and she wouldn't shed another tear over him, not after tonight.

She stood silently for a moment beneath the streetlight with it's bowed head illuminating the night. The last flutters of snow sputtered to the ground and the final police car pulled around the corner and out of sight.

For the first time in five years, Vera felt that things were going to change for the better. She pulled the coat around her more tightly and returned to the house.

"You alright?" Paul asked. He had been standing on the porch smoking a cigarette.

There was a slight shake in his hand and she knew that it wasn't just from the cold.

She nodded and hugged him. She couldn't remember ever hugging him before, and it had caught him off guard. After a brief moment he returned the embrace.

"Thank you." she said.

"You're welcome."

Vera had broken sleep that night. She dreamed of screaming men and charging trucks. She dreamt of murder and pain. In the dark, alone and unknowing, she cried in her sleep.

VERA

Vera Daniels was lost.

After her divorce, having to rebuild seemed like an endless daunting task that she could not deal with.

"Here on vacation?" the woman asked Vera as she turned the hand crank that propelled them across the crystal clear water. The woman had startled her from her daydream.

Vera nodded, "Something like that."

Every "must visit" list had included Kitch-Iti-Kipee on their list and she now understood why. The crystal clear waters stretched two-hundred feet across and nearly fifty feet deep in complete transparency. She could see the enormous lake trout below swaying in serene silence. She envied the complete silence that surely engulfed their alien world below the surface. The spring that fed the spectacle bubbled ferociously at the bottom, stirring the sand into a maelstrom of movement that looked out of place in the depths of the glass-smooth surface.

"Most everyone here is," The woman said, still cranking the lever that would take the platform across the water, sending smooth concentric circles spreading out over it.

She had crossed the Mackinaw Bridge the day before, it's enormous support beams stretching into the sky, wrapped in cables which suspended it five-hundred feet above the cool waters where Lake Michigan and Lake Huron met in the straits below. Her father had once told her of a woman that had lost her life when the Yugo subcompact she had been driving was struck by a gust of wind, hurling the vehicle over the edge of the bridge. No one saw it happen and it was decades before her watery grave was discovered. Vera shivered and was thankful for the weight of her Jeep Wrangler as the tires rumbled musically over the grates for the five mile stretch of bridge.

She stopped in St. Ignace just north of the bridge when she saw the natural stone structure known as Castle Rock towering above the land, a stone finger pointed towards the heavens. At the base had been a massive plaster statue of the Midwest legend Paul Bunyan, accompanied by his always faithful companion Babe the Blue Ox. She entered through the gift shop, filled with the knick-knack variety of keepsakes and curios that brought the tourists in droves during the summer months. She would most likely hand over cash at the end of her journey for one of these, just like thousands of others would.

The walk to the top had been exhausting and her thighs burned by the time she reached the apex of the natural wonder. She could see for miles in every direction, the summer sun happily licking at her skin in warm strokes as she gazed in wonder at the massive freighters filled with ore and other unknown resources, watching as they disappeared slowly over the horizon.

She spent the previous night sleeping in the driver seat of the Wrangler, parking it in the lot of a mom-and-pop grocery store. She had noted the lack of chain stores the further north her trek had taken her. It was strange to see a world before Wal-Mart and Whole Foods, almost as if she had traveled through a wormhole in the space-time continuum to a simpler past. Her slumber had been disturbed by the dreams that had haunted her since the assault two winters prior. The screaming, the truck, the gunshots, all came back in vivid detail when she closed her eyes and dozed.

Some nights the dreams didn't come, but those days were few and far between. She may have divorced Craig, but she couldn't escape her own mind. In there he still kept her company, laying in wait and ready to strike around every corner and from every patch of darkness.

"Excuse me."

The man had interrupted her thoughts, startling her.

"Oh, sorry didn't mean to scare you, miss."
He smiled. She returned the smile nervously.
He asked, "Would you mind taking a picture
of us please?"

He gestured at a woman that was clearly
his wife. Her red hair caught the sun, giving
it a gorgeous glow and she flashed a toothy
smile at Vera and nodded a hello. The little
girl in her arms was oblivious to the
introductions, staring cautiously at one of
the herons that honked loudly from the bank.

"Oh, it's okay," said Vera, "I was just
daydreaming. Yeah, of course I'll take your
picture."

He gave her a quick run-through of the
camera, which was unnecessary. It was of
the 'point and shoot' variety. His wife

wrangled two boys,- about five and eight years old- away from the edge and told them to pose for the picture. The younger boy had hair to match his mother's and freckles peppered his nose. The other was a miniature carbon copy of his father with handsome dark hair and blue eyes.

They smiled- the red headed boy flexing his muscles adorably instead- as she snapped the photograph. "Thank you," the woman said gratefully, "It's our first trip with the kids and we've been trying to get pictures for the scrapbook."

"You have a lovely family," Said Vera, not completely without envy. She and Craig had talked about having children many times, but despite not using contraceptives it had never happened. Probably for the best, all things considered, Vera thought.

"I'm six!" said the red headed boy, holding up his hands to display six tiny raised fingers.

"Six!" Vera exclaimed dramatically in false disbelief, "Six whole years? You're almost a grown up!"

The boy laughed and shook his head furiously, "I'm not a grown up! I'm just Tyler!"

Tyler darted off laughing to the edge of the platform, trying to see the fish most liekly, but his brother lingered behind, curious about the strange woman that his parents were talking to.

"And who are you?" Vera asked him. Rose-colored circles appeared high on his cheeks.

"Bryant." He almost whispered.

"He's our shy one." Said their mother tousling his hair playfully, "I'm Marjorie Denham. This is my husband Chris."

Vera shook their hands. It was nice to see that not everyone in the world were bitter and heartless drones that feared interacting with other humans.

"First time here?" Chris asked her.

"Yeah, the furthest north I've ever been until yesterday was Mackinaw City," she answered, "It's so gorgeous up here!"

"We're on our way home to Lansing. We stayed for a week in Copper Harbor, figured we would stop off on the way home and show the kids this place. We stopped here a few times before any of them were born, but it wasn't as well kept back then." Said Marjorie, hushing the toddler who had now grown bored of their adventure.

"Really cleaned the place up." Said Chris, "Not to mention that tourists such as ourselves have really increased their budget up here."

Vera had inadvertently caught the little girl's attention and she now smiled cautiously at Vera, her hand opening and closing in an awkward wave.

"Hello, little one." Vera said, waving back. The girl grasped her hand and squeezed it, happily cooing.

"Looks like Marie likes you!" Marjorie chuckled. Marie stretched out her arms towards Vera in the universal kid signal for 'pick me up'.

"Do you mind?" Vera asked the mother, who shook her head as she handed the girl over. Marie grasped lightly at Vera's hair and smiled again, a laugh escaping from her chubby belly as she flailed her free hand excitedly.

"Kids of your own?" Chris asked as he snapped a picture of the heron that had been entertaining his daughter.

"No," said Vera as she booped Marie's nose playfully, bringing on another wave of chubby giggles, "My ex-husband and I talked a lot about it, but it just never happened."

"That's too bad," said Marjorie, frowning slightly, "It suits you."

Marie had had enough of Vera and was clawing the air in the direction of her mother, "Kid, you really gotta start walking soon, you're killing my back." Said Marjorie.

Marie answered by yanking at the tiny hairs on the back of her mother's neck playfully.

"I don't think she's a fan of that idea," said Vera laughing as Marjorie rubbed the spot vigorously in annoyance.

"Where are you heading?" she asked when she had finished.

Vera shrugged, "I'm not really sure yet. I was thinking about camping out a few nights or maybe hiking Ottawa National Forest."

Chris jerked his head in her direction, his attention pulled from his photography, "Did you say hiking the National Forest?"

"Yeah, my mom did it when she was younger and I thought it sounded interesting."

He looked nervously at Marjorie and then continued cautiously, "You need to be careful up here. There are all kinds of things out in those woods." He said, "I'm not trying to scare you off from it, but if it's not bears, wolves, or mountain lions, it's the fucking tweakers cooking meth out there."

"Dear!" hissed Marjorie, "Language! And mind your own business."

He shrugged, "What, you'd rather her not know about it?"

"My dad grew up around Marquette," said Vera, laughing,   "He already gave me the heads up and tried to prepare me as best as he could for it. I can put up my tent in approximately seven minutes now, thanks to him nagging me to death over it.

What she neglected to mention was the Smith and Wesson .45 caliber pistol that her father had insisted she purchase for the trip. He had taken her to the range for three weekends, until she felt comfortable enough shooting the gun, before he had relented. Vera liked the way the gun felt in her hand.

The smell of gunpowder as it created an apocalypse of fire and smoke calmed her in an eerie peaceful way.

Her father had insisted on contributing two pieces of equipment for her trip. One was a flare gun that he had bought for a hunting trip to Montana two years prior, the other was his US Marine issued Ka-Bar knife.

He had been issued the knife before leaving for leaving for the war, and had carried the 7 inch blade with him nearly everywhere since. He'd even kept it in the inner pocket of his tuxedo on his wedding day. Its black handle was worn from use but the matte-finished blade was well kept and razor-sharp. It looked mean in its leather sheath and Vera thought the jagged shark teeth near the handle could have cut bone clean through.

The knife scared her. Not because she was unfamiliar with handling knives, she had handled plenty over the years. She feared that knife because it had seen combat and was engineered specifically to end lives. That knife had probably taken lives.

Vera never asked her father about the war, whether he had killed anyone. She never planned to either, that was between him and the big man upstairs. The knife had given her the answers she had been too afraid to ask:

"You ever gotta use it, go deep and twist." He had said.

"It's a different world up there, Vera," he had said, "You never know what's coming and you'll be miles away from anyone if anything goes wrong. You get in trouble; you pull that trigger until it clicks."

She had sensed his trepidation about the trip, but he remained tight-lipped about it. She knew his worry came from a place of love, stemming from his fear of losing her after the incident with Craig. She had to stop her father from killing Craig the day he was released from jail. He'd gotten off with just a disturbing the peace charge, the lucky bastard. The lawyers had convinced the judge to drop the assault charges for a 'lack of evidence'. She thought her wounds had been evidence enough.

"Are you in a hurry today?" Marjorie asked, snapping Vera back to reality.

"Hurry? No, I have nowhere to be. Just wandering." She answered.

"You should join us for dinner," Marjorie mused, "We're going to grill out in the parking lot when we get back. We've got steak, burgers, and hot dogs, plus all the fixings to go with them."

"Oh, I couldn't-" Vera began to say but was interrupted by Marjorie.

"You can and you will!" she said, "We have plenty enough to go around and if little Marie here likes you, you can't be all bad. I insist."

Chris manned the grill that he set up at the entrance to their fifth-wheel camper, an enormous thing that took up five parking spaces that it was parked across, while Marjorie and Vera removed the husks from the corn. The two boys ran wildly through the open area near the gift shop, occasionally soaring wildly on their stomachs on the swings that had been installed in the park to assist parents with children who were less enthusiastic about natural wonders. Marie sat happily in a lawn chair, distracted by the upside-down book in her lap that she was pretending to read.

Vera had at first been guarded when Marjorie asked what she was doing in the U.P. by herself, but eventually she had told her the story. She had left out some details, like the night Craig had tried to kill her and her family, but gave her the gist of it. Marjorie had listened wide eyed, occasionally interjecting with an "Oh my god!" or "You've gotta be shitting me!"

"Language, dear." Chris had called out sarcastically as he had wandered by at the opportune moment. Marjorie flashed him the finger, grinning.

"Be careful where you point that thing!" He said, swatting her on the butt with the spatula playfully.

"Boys, you be careful and stay out of the road!" Marjorie yelled after Tyler and Bryant, then under her breath, "Little hellions is what they are."

"Good kids though." Vera said, watching as Tyler dumped a handful of the sand beneath the swings into Bryant's dark hair.

"When they want to be."

Dinner was phenomenal and the company was even better. Chris had turned out to be quite the chef.

"You know your way around a piece of meat, Chris!" Vera said, and realized all too late what she had said. Marjorie shot soda from her nose in the ensuing laughter, tears streaming down her face as she giggled herself into breathlessness. They discovered that they lived about an hour away from each other-downstate, The Denhams in Lansing, Vera in Fenton, just south of Flint.

"We'll have to stay in touch!"
Marjorie said. Vera hoped that they would.
She liked all of them, even Chris with his
smart-assed remarks and dorky mannerisms.

"Vera, do you want to play tag with
us?" called Bryant. The two boys had
inhaled their food at an alarming speed,
anxious to get back to their playing, "Tyler
is 'it'."

She joined them, darting between the
swings as Tyler gave chase, his awkward
feet sometimes catching one behind the
other, sending him sprawling to the ground
as he laughed uncontrollably.
 He tricked her by feigning injury, slapping
her on the leg and yelling, "You're it!"
before hauling ass away from her and hiding

behind the bushes lining the gift shop where she couldn't fit.

"Kids!" yelled Chris, "We gotta hit the road! I gotta work Monday morning and we still have a long drive to go!"

"Aw, dad!" said Tyler sadly, his bottom lip stuck out in devastated fashion.

"Let's move it!" Marjorie chimed in, settling the matter before it had a chance to escalate into tantrums.

"Bye, boys." Vera said, still catching her breath as she hugged Marjorie, waving over her shoulder at them, "Be good for your mom or you'll have me to answer to!"

"I'll send them with you," joshed Marjorie, "You be careful out there, okay? Chris wasn't wrong when he said that there are things and people out there that can hurt you."

Vera nodded, "I will be. This is just something I have to do, if that makes sense."

"I know what you mean," said Marjorie as she climbed into the cab of the truck, slamming the door behind her.

"Hey, take it easy on the door!" Chris exclaimed, wagging his finger at Marjorie.

"Well if you would fix the latch I wouldn't have to slam it!" she said, and swatted at him lightly in the driver seat.

"You have my number, right?" Vera asked.

"Already put it in my phone. Be safe!"

"Always." Vera said, waving.

She was saddened to see them pull away, the massive camper in tow. They were a nice family, and those were great kids. The boys had given her a run for her money in their game of tag and she felt her calves burning with overuse and that little girl had melted her heart. She took one last look over her shoulder at the clear waters that had introduced them before climbing into the Wrangler and put it into drive. She only briefly noted the Blazer that had sat quietly in the corner of the lot unnoticed started its engine as she passed by, and forgot about it completely when she input the location of the campground into her GPS.

The route to the campground wound through back roads and overgrown snowmobile trails. At one point the GPS simply showed that she was no longer on a road that it recognized and on the monitor it looked as though she were just a blue arrow in the middle of space.

"Talk about the middle of nowhere," she said to herself, as her Jeep climbed over a sandy hill that she wasn't sure was even a road.

"Rerouting. Rerouting. Rerouting." The GPS kept repeating.

"Jesus, I hear you!" she said, turning the volume down on it with a swipe of her hand. She passed by houses in varying states of either destruction or construction, some looked old and weathered against the elements that went from one extreme to another between winters and summers, others still being built by those who had tired of civilization's burden and wanted a more reclusive life, possibly a summer cabin.

She almost gave up hope of finding the campground after driving through six inches of muddy water that covered the narrow dirt road but after a couple hundred more yards she spied the wooden sign signaling that he had reached the state campground. It was empty save for one dusty white fifth-wheel that was discolored an ugly smoker's yellow. She saw no sign of the occupants and with no vehicle in sight, she assumed the campground was all hers. She filed out the necessary information at the unattended check-in station and dropped several bills into the sealed tube where the camping fee

was kept until a park ranger could gather
them at a later date.

The mosquitoes tried to dampen her spirits,
whining their wings in her ears, but after
tiring of slapping herself silly trying to
vanquish them, she covered herself in the
industrial strength bug repellent that her
father had recommended to her and banished
them back to the hell they had come from.
She made camp quickly, having mastered
her tent at the insistence of her father, and
before long had a fire burning, over which
she cooked one of the steaks that she had
purchased the previous night before falling
asleep in the parking lot of the grocery store.
The cooler had kept it edible and because
she had spent the extra money for a high-end

cooler, she still had plenty of ice to keep the rest of her food fresh as well.

In the darkness that had slowly crept into camp, she didn't see the Blazer that had come in through the back entrance, prowling slowly with its lights off. It parked on the far side of the small pond, which lay in the middle of the campground. It cut its engine off and sat in the inky black unseen, two red dots glowed in the front seats like tamed fireflies held in the hands of beasts.

The crickets rose in a chorus of deafening volume, the frogs soon joined the orchestration and seemed to duet on the off beat of the crickets chirrups. Vera had never seen stars like the ones in the sky tonight. They burned bright, devoid of the light pollution that came with the suburban sprawl of the Lower Peninsula. She felt insignificant in the universe at that very moment as she sipped whiskey from the bottle and staring into the heavens above.

Chapter Three

Vera woke to the sound of starlings just outside her tent. Their tiny shadows bounded happily through the grass as the sun projected them on the side of her tent and grinned when they dive-bombed each other in little kamikaze dips. She woke only twice during the night, maybe the best sleep she had gotten since the night craig lost his mind. The dreams were still there, but not as frequent. They were still terrifying.

She stepped from the tent, stretching as she did, and saw that during the night or incredibly early that morning someone company had joined the campground. A small individual tent sat across the large pond that the campground encircled with a winding hardpan path. No vehicle sat at the campsite, but a woman about fifteen or twenty years her senior sat near the fire. She waved at Vera and smiled. Vera returned the wave. The woman beckoned her toward her enthusiastically, metal coffee pot raised high.

"Hey there, stranger!" the woman said brightly as Vera neared her campsite. The morning dew jostled about in the tall grass, and she could feel the dampness through her pajama pants.

"Hey! Vera Daniels!" she said, extending her hand.

"Valerie Jenkins, please, sit down." she said, gesturing at what seemed to be half of a yoga mat laying near the fire, "Coffee?"

"Yes, please," said Vera. She noted the woman's tangled gray hair and clothes that didn't quite match, as if she had gotten dressed in the dark.

The woman reached into the hiking pack that lay beside her and produced a tin cup. She rinsed it quickly with a splash from a bottle of water and poured the steaming liquid into it.

"Sugar?" she asked, displaying several packets of the sweet stuff. Vera took two and stirred them in with a clean-looking stick she found on the ground.

Vera sipped it. It was instant, but still delicious and warmed her belly.

"What are you doing here all by your lonesome?" Valerie asked, eyebrows raised in genuine interest.

"It's kind of complicated." Vera said. She didn't feel like telling a complete stranger all of her woes.

"Ah," said Valerie, "Man problems." Then laughed at the look of gobsmacked surprise on Vera's face.

"Well, not exactly, but close enough. How did you know?" Vera asked. The air was chilly and she warmed her hands on the tin mug.

"Lucky guess." Valere said, pouring herself a second cup.

"What about you?" Vera asked, crossing her legs indian style.

"Honey, that is a LONG story." laughed the woman

Vera insisted, "I've got nothing but time and would love to hear it."

The woman pulled a book from her pack, followed by a large prescription medicine bottle. She laid the book across her lap and opened the bottle, sprinkling several chunks of leafy green buds across it. She began to roll a joint after pulling a pack of rolling papers from her pocket and plucking one free.

"Well," Valerie began, "My husband and I used to come up here every year- we owned a cabin just south of Marquette."

She lit the joint and inhaled quickly several times, stoking the cherry to stay burning. She did all of this with expert flair, as if smoking had been a long-time hobby or a full-time job.

"We used to have so much fun together, wandering around and getting lost. He always seemed to be able to find the way we needed though. 'Just follow the sun' he would say. I never got the hang of it, you could have dropped me in my backyard and I would get lost, I swear."

"Me too!"

She offered Vera the joint. She considered and then took it. It burned her lungs and she tried to hold in the cough but failed. Eyes watering, she passed it back.

"You gotta cough to get off, sweety." Valerie laughed heartily. She had a great laugh, one that was infectious and bubbly. The lines in her faced deepened with her smile.

"It's been years since I've smoked that," said Vera, fighting the urge to gag at a cough, "But what the hell, right?"

"Right!" Valerie said, "We used to travel all over in our motorhome, we bought one off of a neighbor in the summer of '92 or '93. We took that damn thing all over:

The Grand Canyon, The Rockies, Yosemite, Yellowstone. A lot of great memories in that beat up old thing. It finally gave up on us shortly after Tom got his diagnosis."

"Cancer?" Vera asked. It was almost always cancer.

Valerie pursed her lips and nodded, "Cancer indeed. Prostate. He went downhill quickly after that. It was already at Stage Four when we found out. It takes a lot to come back from that and he was already too far gone by the time her got it checked out. I tried to tell him, but you know how men are." Her eyes were glistening.

"You loved him very much, didn't you?"

"I loved him more than there are stars in the universe, honey." said Valerie, wiping a singular tear that escaped her wrinkled eye, "But that's why we lose people, y'know? So we know how strong love truly is. You don't know love until you lose the one and feel that deep ache in your chest, the pit of your stomach."

Vera thought of Craig. She hadn't felt that pit when they had ended their marriage. She had felt relief.

"After that, things kinda got wonky for me." Valerie said as she exhaled a large cloud of smoke, "Without his income- I was a stay at home wife the bank took the house, the cars, pretty much everything. We never had kids- though we tried- so I was on my own."

"I can't imagine." Vera said. She felt sorry for the woman. She seemed genuine and tough, but sweet as could be. Those blue eyes still sparkled with life and happiness whenever she still smiled- which was often- but there was still a deep hurt within her.

"You don't want to imagine that. I did what we did best," said Valerie, "I drifted. Made my way south to Florida for a few years and made a few friends there. There was this one fella in Miami that was sweet on me for awhile, but it just wasn't the same as with Tom. That ended when he beat me up one night when I told him we needed to end things."

Vera didn't need to imagine that part. "That's how my marriage ended. He attacked me when he got the divorce papers. He would have murdered me if my family and the police hadn't stopped him."

Valerie stubbed out the small portion of joint that remained into the dirt and pocketed the remains, "Funny how that happens, ain't it? They love you so much that they'll do their worst?"

"That's really the reason that I needed to come up here for awhile and clear my head." said Vera tugging at the tall grass absentmindedly, "I had about a months worth of vacation time, so I said 'to hell with it" and took it. I thought about the Caribbean, but that seemed more of a couples thing. My mom always talked about the U.P. and a trip she had up here after college, just after she met my dad. I decided to follow in her footsteps and get lost for a bit."

"You came to the right place to get lost." Valerie said matter-of-factly, "Lost is pretty much all their is up here."

"What did you do next?" Vera asked, genuinely interested in the woman's story.

"I got out while the gettin' was good. Right after I left the hospital, that is. Spent a week in there with all kinds of hoses and tubes attached to me, he got me good. The police didn't arrest him because they labeled it as a 'domestic dispute' and they are hesitant to prosecute those kinds of things."

The sun had risen higher in the sky and the warmth was welcome in the chilly morning. The frogs had begun their morning tune and the two women listened silently to them for a moment.

Valerie cleared her throat and went on, "I wound up in Texas living in a camp with a group of others. Rough around the edges crowd but good people that took care of each other when someone needed it."

"You lived in a campground?" Vera queried.

Valerie smiled and shook her head, "No, honey. I lived in a homeless camp."

It suddenly all made sense the Vera. The mismatched clothes that didn't match or seem to fit right, the patched more than it should have been tent, the lack of a vehicle, the hiking pack. "You're homeless?" she asked, heartbroken.

"You didn't pick up on that sooner? Good lord, honey, look at me!" Valerie laughed, running her hands along the frame of her body as if to say, "Are you fucking blind?"

"I'm sor-" Vera began to apologize but Valerie stopped her with a raised hand.

"There is no need to be sorry! I've enjoyed my life and my travels. There have been-" she tumbled her head side to side, "rough patches? But for the most part? I wouldn't change a thing!"

Vera chewed nervously at her lip, unsure of what to say.

"The homeless get a bad reputation," Valerie mused, "They try to keep us hidden away. They'll kick you off of the bench you're sleeping on just so you don't ruin a person's day by being poor, or mentally ill, dirty or just a little weird. But if I'm really being honest, some of the best people I've ever met didn't have a pot to piss in or a window to throw it out off."

"Weren't you scared?"

"Of being on my own without a home?" said Valerie, her eyebrows once again raised, "You're damn right I was scared! I made do with what I could and learned the tricks along the way."

"I don't think I could do it," Vera said, "I don't think I have those kind of instincts in me."

Valerie scoffed a laugh, "Oh, you would survive. When you get desperate and hungry, you'd be surprised what some people would do. The instincts are in there, they're in all of us. It's just a matter of desperation. That's the driving force for some people, Vera: desperation."

Vera could not fathom the tenacity that Valerie must have to still be as chipper and bubbly as she was. She seemed slightly eccentric, but in a good way. She reminded Vera of a teacher that she had in middle school that sang every instruction that she ever gave. The joke among the kids in her class was that she would even scold you with a song. This theory had turned out to be horrible false when they witnessed her finally snap and scream red-faced and shaking at Ryan Elsworth when he had placed a tack in her seat. Vera could still remember the look of surprise on the woman's face when she had sat on it. It could still make her laugh some days.

"What brought you up this way?" Vera asked, abandoning the grass she had been fidgeting with after realizing she had been fidgeting. It was one of her biggest pet peeves.

"I come up here once a year to scatter some of Tom's ashes." Valerie said, her hand rubbing the large pendant that hung round her neck on a piece of rawhide leather string, "I think this might be the last year for that. Starting to run low on him."

With that she tapped the pendant and Vera saw that it wasn't just a fashion statement. It had a screw-top on top of the pewter heart-shaped piece. It was a miniature urn holding the last of the woman's husband.

"Did you come from downstate?" she asked.

"No, I was in Milwaukee. Caught a few rides.

An eighteen wheeler dropped me off on the highway and I walked the last couple of miles. Some days I walked though. My legs aren't quite what they used to be at my age. Forty five is *not* the new twenty." Valerie said, rolling her eyes with thick amounts of sarcasm, "I've experienced it first hand and forty five is definitely forty five."

Vera guessed she was fifteen or twenty years older but the road had aged the woman, she was older by only a decade. She was thin, but not gaunt, from miles walked and the lack of consistent diet. Her hair had grayed prematurely and she wore it long and wild; Vera guessed that she had been blonde before it had. She wasn't a gorgeous woman, but had been pretty once upon a time, and her eyes and smile still showed that beauty.

"There's more stories to tell," Valerie said, "but I think that's enough for now, don't you?"

Vera could have listened to Valerie reminisce on her past and stories for the remainder of the day had it not been for the growing hunger in her stomach. It growled audibly.

"Oh, excuse me," Vera laughed embarrassed, "I haven't had breakfast yet. Have you?"

Valerie shook her head and raised her arms as if to say, "What are you gonna do?"

Vera had seen a diner five miles down the highway the previous night and asked the woman if she wanted to go get breakfast, her treat. Valerie had declined at first, but at Vera's insistence she agreed.

"Should we pack up the tents?" Vera asked.

"I think I'm going to be staying here for another night or two, but feel free to pack up yours if you'd like."

Vera did, carefully putting each tent leg and stake in the proper bags the way her father had drilled into her head. Double checking her area for any trash that may have found its way out of the car and finding nothing but a couple of cigarette butts. She hadn't smoked the previous night and they weren't her brand, but she picked them up anyways. She planned to travel further north and west, closer to Ottawa National Forest today, maybe stopping at any places that looked interesting or odd every once in awhile. A nice easy driving day.

The diner was open, although only two customers sat drinking coffee in a corner booth. Two log trucks were parked outside and Vera correctly assumed that they were the drivers, stopping for a quick meal before sleeping through the day in their cab and traveling at night. They grumbled for more coffee.

The food was delicious and home cooked. They smiled over a *real* cup of coffee, Valerie smacking her lips in delight.

"Want some pie for dessert?" Vera asked her, pointing toward the glass case near the door that housed at least two dozen different varieties.

"Honey, you know it." said Valerie, laughing loudly in excitement. It had probably been years since she a slice of pie, Vera thought not without a sense of sadness at the thought.

They finished their meal, and with bellies full, returned to the campground.

"Want to smoke before you leave?" Valerie asked, thumbing at her tent.

Vera- who was still as high as a kite from the last time they had smoked- declined politely.

"Where you headed next?" Vera asked her, "Do you have a phone or anything?"

Valerie shook her head, "No phone but I do have an email address that I can check once in awhile. I like to visit the libraries sometimes and catch up on the news I've missed. As far as where I'm going? Who knows, maybe California, maybe Boston? The world is my oyster, doll."

They shared a long hug and shared goodbyes, wishing each other luck in their journeys, Valerie putting her email address into Vera's phone, at first struggling with the touch screen, "These damn things are garbage." she had said plainly, "What's wrong with perfectly good buttons."

 Vera climbed into the Jeep to leave, Valerie walking the path back to her tent.

Before she could shut the door, Valerie's arm shot up, finger raised, as if she had remembered something and she spun around with a little shuffling-run, "I almost forgot!" Vera poked her head out of the Jeep, "Forgot what?"

"This morning when I was setting up my tent! I had meant to tell you and forgot completely." Valerie said, thumping herself in the forehead lightly, "I had just gotten here, it was still dark but you could see the sun starting to lighten the sky a little. There was an SUV of some kind parked over there," she pointed to left side of the pond furthest from their end, "an older looking one. There were two men inside of it smoking cigarettes and tossing them out the window. Just sittin' there in the dark with the car off. Kinda gave me the willies for a minute."

Vera hadn't seen another vehicle when she had passed that end of the lake the previous night and she thought it strange, but not worth mentioning. It was probably just two guys catching some shuteye real quick, or maybe two lovers. The Upper Peninsula was quite conservative and things of that nature were still typically taboo in some counties. "Now, I can't be sure, obviously, but I think they were watching your tent." Valerie said, "But something in my gut tells me that they were. You watch yourself out here, Vera."

"Why would someone want to watch my tent?" Vera asked, but goose bumps ran down her arms in spite of the ever-warming sun.

Valerie looked down her nose at Vera- those eyebrows ever raised, "Honey, you know the *many* reasons why they could be doing that and can you think of a single one that isn't terrible?"

Vera could not. She was too busy thinking about the cigarette butts that she had found around her campsite.

Chapter Four

The hour drive to Munising went by in a
blur. She kept checking the rearview,
waiting to see a vehicle following her every
twist and turn. She stopped for coffee and to
stretch her legs at the halfway point, pulling
into the empty parking lot of a diner very
much like the one she had visited earlier in
the day with Valerie. These roadside eateries
tended to become the same in her mind; the

glass dessert cases, taxidermy on the walls, and small novelty rack complete with postcards.

She paid for the coffee and cautiously stepped through the door, glancing around the parking lot. It was empty. If someone had been watching her, they were long gone by now.

She felt slight relief at this, and the remaining drive was much more enjoyable being able to focus on the roadside views, as opposed to the compulsive checking of mirrors and looking for phantom stalkers.

She arrived at the boat launch twenty minutes before they were set to leave the docks, making sure to grab the ticket from her purse and tucking a few twenties into her front pocket. Grabbing a hoodie from the back of the Jeep- it tended to be breezy on the water- she headed for the boat.

The Pictured Rocks were one of the largest tourist attractions in Michigan, thousands of people flocked to the Munising area every year to gaze at the bare cliff faces worn away by wind and waters of Lake Superior over the course of existence. They burned brilliant red and yellows as the sun reflected from the iron, sandstone, copper, and other minerals that gave them their exceptional colors. Small caves were visible at the base of the cliffs, filling with water with every lap of the waves, sending water jetting back out when they had been filled beyond capacity.

She could have taken a kayak, but venturing into the waters alone in such a small craft was not the ideal situation with the threat of overturning and the unlikely event of a cliff collapse- which *was* a yearly occurrence along the shoreline.

Her favorite moment of the tour had been when the boat pulled into a massive alcove, filling the void with their two story vessel. She heard several children on the deck below scream with fear thinking that they would strike the walls and sink to a watery grave, like those unfortunate souls that lay in the wreckage in hundreds of shipwrecks along this coast. The crew laughed as they reversed from the crevice, having performed the feat thousands of times for millions of people over the decade, it was business as usual for them.

Seasonal waterfalls poured from the rocks and surged into the blue waters below, churning foam with the incredible power they exerted, the tallest being Bridal Veil Falls at nearly 150 feet in a sliding plunge to the lake. She saw hikers standing above, waving at the boats with cameras in hand. She returned their waves and snapped her own pictures.

Her parents had been right. This place had a magic to it that demanded to be seen, as if the earth was speaking to the viewers of her wonders, *"See all that I am capable of, the beauty and destruction."*

Lunch was sounding more and more like a good idea by the time the three-hour boat tour had ended. She bought several keepsake items from the gift shop before leaving the lakeshore, heading south towards the interior of the peninsula.

The clouds had begun to thicken and it looked for awhile as if it may rain, but cleared late in the afternoon as Vera made camp. Tomorrow she would make it to Ottawa National Forest, but for the time being she would be staying at another of the rural state campsites, this one lodged far back off of the highway. She had to stop and check her road map several times to find it, the GPS had lost service in this dead zone, but eventually she reached the ten-site campground with slightly higher blood pressure and the need for a cigarette. It had taken several hours longer than planned. Perhaps it was just coincidence, but Vera couldn't shake the feeling of being watched for the rest of the day. She sped north, passing through small towns and villages that looked caught in the last decade rather than the present. Valerie's story had unnerved her and finding the fresh cigarette butts had fed those fears.

The campground was empty, save for a smoker's-yellow fifth wheel that looked like it belonged in the previous decade. The paint was chipped in places and a dark green tarp was strung over the top as if the roof would spring leaks if it were to rain. She saw no sign of activity near the camper and assumed that the owners were either out seeing the sights or had possibly abandoned it. With the shape it was in, she could easily see the latter being a real possibility.

Her cell had service, which had surprised her. She hadn't been able to use it for most of the trip but saw two solid bars, meaning a phone call was in the cards. She selected "Home" from her contacts and the phone began to ring. Although she hadn't lived with her parents in over a decade, she still had labeled it that in her phone.

"Hello?" her father answered in a grumble.

"Hey, dad!" Vera said cheerfully.

"Vera! How's the trip? I hope everything is going okay?" He started interrogating,

"Moira pick up the other line it's Vera!" he yelled, forcing Vera to pull the phone from her ear to avoid being deafened.

She filled them in on the trip, telling them about all she had seen and experienced. Her mother hadn't been happy when Vera told them about Valerie. She left out the part about the men watching her tent. She didn't want to worry them.

"She could have been some kind of crazy woman, Vera!" she had said angrily, "For Christ's sake!"

Her father had simply listened and grunted his responses, occasionally asking questions. She knew the trip was still a sore subject for him.

They spoke only for a few minutes before Vera told them she had to set up camp and needed to let them go.

"Be careful out there, and make sure you keep that gun on your hip at all times! We're an open carry state and you should take advantage of it!" her father said in a demand more than suggestion.

"I will, dad!"

Setting up camp took only several minutes and she found that she had time to stroll the area before dark crept in and swallowed the sun.

She found herself reading the signs at the check-in station, coming across an orange sheet of paper with a picture of a bear on it,

one she hadn't seen when she paid the fee
upon arriving.

"WARNING:

Bears have been spotted in this area.
Please be cautious of your surroundings and
do not engage the animal. Please make sure
to keep all trash and food in a scent-proof
container and locked away if possible. If a
bear approaches you, make your presence
known with calm, relaxing tones. Back away
slowly from the animal and walk, DO NOT
RUN. Keep your eye on the bear to make
sure it is not becoming aggressive-"

It continued on but she did not finish the
article. She'd read all of the bear safety she
had wanted to read when researching for her

trip. Bears were far less worrisome to her than other humans.

She returned to camp, and after eating, read for several hours by the light of her lantern before turning in early.

Vera jerked violently awake at the rumble of an engine as a vehicle passed near her tent. For a brief moment she knew it was Craig coming to finish the job, he had found her. The she imagined the two men in the Blazer that Valerie had mentioned, the ones watching her tent as she slept, smoking cigarettes as they circled her like sharks in the night. Her senses came back to her and she peeked an eye through one of the barely-unzipped

windows of the tent and saw the beat up, rusted box-style Chevrolet pull up next to the trailer she had thought was abandoned. The exhaust hung lazily from the bed, bowing low and nearly touching the ground as it bounced over the ruts.

She glanced at her watch. 3 am. Hell of a time to be returning to camp with an exhaust as loud as that. Two men climbed out of the truck and she heard the tinkling of beer cans tumbling to the ground. The image of Craig shambling out of the Skylark flashed like a neon sign in her memory.

"Time to get to work!" one yelled, stretching with exaggeration.

"Shut up, Errol!" said the other, pointing in the direction of her tent. Vera froze. She was too scared to blink, to breathe.

"Oh!" said the one named Errol excitedly, "Company, Davey!"

The man made toward her tent in a happy jaunt.

"No. We're here to do a job, and we're going to do it." said Davey, "You can do your own thing when you aren't getting paid to do another!"

"Fine," said Errol, sounding like a child that had just received a scolding and was now pouting as he returned to the truck, shoulders slumped in defeat

Vera tried to slow her breathing, afraid they would hear her nervous inhales and exhales in the silence. They stared at her tent for several minutes before Davey spoke up, "Alright, let's do this."

The sound of a generator tore through the night and the lights of the trailer blinked into existence. Vera saw the two men more clearly now, both large and looming figures in the dark. The one called Errol kept staring intently every couple of seconds at her tent, she saw the cherry of his cigarette bobbing from his side to his mouth and then back again.

"Move your ass!" yelled Davey over the generator, opening the door to the trailer. Vera couldn't see inside but he had a good idea of what they were going to be doing in it. Her mind raced for a plan. She could stay and risk whatever Errol had wanted to do to her, or she could try to pack up as silently as possible and get the hell out of here before they finished what they were doing.

As quietly as possible she began rolling her sleeping bag into the neat roll it had come in. She flinched at every click of the zipper as she worked it along the track silently. She was worried about one of them appearing unannounced in the darkness- she was unable to hear the sound of the door to the camper opening over the sound of the generator. She created a gap large enough to poke her head through, sure one of them would snatch her as she did, but to her relief she could clearly see both of them through the now-lit windows of the trailer.

She slipped swiftly but silently out of the tent carrying the sleeping bag, shuffling slowly through the dark to the Wrangler and tried the handle. Locked. The keys were in the pants she had been wearing before changing into her pajamas.

"Shit!" she whispered to herself angrily.

She retrieved the keys and not thinking, opened the Wrangler door. The dome light kicked on, stinging her unadjusted eyes and sending dim beams out the windows. She slapped her hand angrily over the light and switched it to off on the control panel. She sat as quiet as possible, listening for a sign that the men had seen it. They hadn't. The quiet, annoying ding of the open door alarm was unavoidable and she silently prayed that she was able to complete her task before anyone could hear it.

Moving quickly, she disassembled the tent, tossing the pieces into the back seat of the Jeep frantically rather than packing them nicely into their nylon draw-bags as she had during her trial runs. Her breathing was erratic as the anxiety began creeping through her and she had to keep checking compulsively over her shoulder to make sure that no danger was approaching in the darkness.

Maybe she was overreacting or being paranoid, but she didn't want to take any chances of the men getting any ideas about the stranger in the tent next to what was likely their meth lab. That was the conclusion that she came to about what they had been up to, and something deep inside told her that she was correct in her assumptions.

Meth was a popular pastime in this area and those who manufactured it could make a killing from the dealers, or even more if they sold it themselves. The lack of police to patrol the rural areas fueled their bold behaviors.

She tossed the last piece of the tent into the Jeep just as the generator sputtered and stalled. Sprinting to the driver side of the vehicle, she slid into the driver seat, quietly shutting the door as the door to the fifth wheel burst open and the men stepped out, gas masks covering their faces.

She was hoping they wouldn't see that her tent was no longer where it had been when they entered the camper, that the generator would fire back up easily, and they would return to the business they had been conducting. After she watched them pull several times at the cord of the generator, she knew that she would have no such luck.

They removed their gas masks, the taller one of the two, Errol-she thought, pointed to where the tent had been. She couldn't hear the men other than their heavily muffled voices, but took a guess at what they were saying.

"Whoever is over there was awake when we got here, probably knows what we are doing, and needs to be dealt with."

She slipped the key into the ignition and cranked it. She hoped that by leaving slowly and calmly they would think she was just moving on to quieter pastures where a generator would not be humming loudly one-hundred feet away while she was trying to sleep.

She reversed slowly, trying to keep an eye on them in the rearview but losing them when she cranked the wheel to straighten her tires on the hardpan dirt path that served as a road.

"Stay calm." she kept repeating in her head as though it were a meditative mantra. *"You*

don't need to get yourself more worked up than you already are."

When she shifted it into drive she checked the mirror again. They were no longer standing near the generator and she couldn't spot them lurking in any of her blind spots. She edged the car forward through the darkness, not wanting them to feel as though she warranted following. She had made it around the first bend that swept wide right on the winding drive through the campground when she was able to breathe a sigh of relief, although her heart still jack hammered in her chest so hard you could almost see it protruding through it.

That had been enough high-tension for her tonight. She would find another site somewhere further up Highway 2 and sleep in the driver's seat where the door locks offered her some solace, at least for the night. She would try this adventure again tomorrow night, miles away from this place and more importantly, further away from those men.

She swept left around the bend and her headlights caught the legs and torsos of two figures standing in the middle of the path. She rolled to a stop, ten feet from them and seeing them clearly for the first time.

The taller one looked as if he were cut from stone, massive muscle rippled beneath the white tank top, a gigantic scar running diagonally from his right eye to the left corner of his mouth. The other man stood

nearly six inches shorter and was plump.
Long greasy hair dangled at his shoulders.
The grey goatee around his mouth bore a
chewing tobacco stain down the middle.
Both of them wore an empty smile from ear
to ear.

She opened the center console and pulled
out the Smith and Wesson .45, keeping it
low and against her leg.

*"If you get in trouble, squeeze the trigger
until it clicks empty."* her father's voice said
in her mind. She hoped she wouldn't have to
use the gun.

She revved the engine, the Jeep jerking
forward slightly with each touch of the
accelerator. Just when she thought they
weren't going allow her to pass through,

they parted as if they were the gatekeepers of her freedom and had allowed her the luxury. She punched the accelerator and flew between them, swearing she could hear them laughing hysterically as she did.

She saw them staring after her as the taillights illuminated their faces, grins still spread wide. The bumps in the path jarred her violently as she took them faster than was safe. She wanted to put some distance between her and the rednecks that had scared the shit out of her. They were probably just fucking with her, playing a prank or something, but something inside told her that they were up to no good and were dangerous. She learned to listen to her gut instinct by now.

Two miles down the road she paused to catch her breath and to check the GPS. She would see any headlights coming in either direction coming from a long ways off on this straight stretch of road.

She reached into the glove box and pulled out a pack of Marlboro Reds. She rarely smoked anymore unless the anxiety came to be unbearable. Her hand shook as she lit the cigarette, and took a deep drag as she cracked the window a few inches to let the smoke escape in long white strands.

The GPS indicated that fifteen miles north on the highway there would be a rest area where she could rest her eyes for a couple of hours. Safety in numbers and civilization, after all.

Over the hum of her engine she heard two loud pops, they sounded like faint gunshots. They were followed by two more. They had come from the direction she had been traveling from, "Fucking hicks." she said, before stubbing out the cherry of the cigarette on the top of the side-view mirror and put the remaining half between the flip-down visor and the roof of the car.

She wondered nervously if they had the gun with them when they had stopped her. She thought that they had. It sent the hair on the back of her neck on end and she had to rub it to shake the feeling that a goose had just walked over her grave.

The further north she travelled, the more she felt foolish. She likely overreacted, even *if* the men *were* cooking meth. She likely scared the shit out of them just as much as they scared her, and she put money on them having hooked the camper up to the truck after she left and getting while the getting was good. Meth heads were notoriously paranoid as it was without strangers putting them on edge and they wouldn't risk the police busting them by staying where they had been spotted. For all they knew she had already called the police. She already decided that she wouldn't.

She left the window cracked for some fresh air as she cruised up the highway, every now and then braking for a deer and, once, for a moose just south of Marquette. It's massive antlers casting spidery shadows on the blacktop behind it as it crossed slowly, staring at the Jeep every few moments.

"At least you aren't cooking meth or playing with guns, big guy." she said to him, as he cleared the road, vanishing into the trees.

The rest area was well lit, although there were only a handful of cars parked there when she arrived, most of them empty. The tractor-trailer side of the building seemed teeming with movement as the long haul truckers pulled in and out towards sleep or their next delivery respectively.

This would have to do. It was ten after four in the morning and she could barely keep her eyes open. She couldn't believe it had only been an hour since the loud Chevrolet had roared passed her tent like a lion searching for prey.

She knew that because of the night Craig had finally snapped she was more guarded and nervous than others. She knew what kind of things that people were capable of. She knew her friends, or those she had called friends before that night, whispered about how crazy she was.

She heard the rumors about the PTSD that had developed. She wasn't sure if it was PTSD, some days she thought it was and others she thought it was something else, maybe a sixth sense that let her know that something wasn't right in the world.

Maybe she was crazy after all, the nightmares seemed to validate that. They haunted her nearly every night, depriving her of sleep for months on end. Some days she felt like a ghost wandering the world, unseen by those around her.

She lit the half-cigarette and smoked it , walking the concrete path to the rest area bathrooms. It seemed fairly well-kept compared to the ones in the Lower Peninsula, probably because they saw fewer people roll through in these parts. It was possible that people up here had more respect for their surroundings. It was more likely a combination of the two.

She used the restroom and grabbed water from the vending machine, nearly drinking it down in a single go.

Tomorrow would be a better day. She would give her parents a call first thing when she woke up to check in with them and let them know that everything was fine, leaving out the part about the encounter she had just experienced. No need to make them more worried than they already were. Her mom wasn't nearly as worried as her father.

Her mother wanted her to get out and meet new people as soon as her divorce was finalized. She couldn't understand how someone could be comfortable being alone, and it had taken Vera months to convince her mother that she wouldn't be seeing anyone for the foreseeable future.

Her mentioning the trip was her sly way of trying to plant the seed of adventure in

Vera's mind, and it had succeeded with the vivid descriptions of the landscapes, cliffs and gullies that peppered the peninsula.

Chapter Five

Her sleep in the rest area was broken and
filled with dreams of headlights chasing her
through the darkness. Just before they
reached her she would jump herself awake
as if she dreamed of falling. She once read a
study somewhere that claimed that feeling
was the brain making sure the body wasn't
dying. The sound of the semi-trucks hissing
their brakes stabbed through the night in a

serpent's hiss, like a steam engine releasing great plumes of vapor.

Abandoning the prospect of sleep at the first sign of sunlight, she pulled the Jeep onto the highway and headed southwest toward the national forest. Towns grew fewer and further in between, and the cellular service was non-existent in the expanse of wilderness that now surrounded the black stretch of road before her. The traffic, although it had already been near-empty roadways, vanished to the point that she was surprised when another car appeared in the oncoming lane.

She felt like she was traveling through a desolate wasteland in an alternate future where nature has reclaimed the land from the grips of the madmen that sought to damage it. It was an awe-inspiring feeling that she had never before experienced.

Nature had won the battle here, except against the most hardened and recluse. You could disappear here completely. The last gas station she stopped at didn't even have the ability to accept credit or debit.

"Cash only." the man tending the station said when she attempted to hand him her card.

He looked at her with distrust, the way that locals in any small town look at outsiders, a look that said, "*You are not one of us, so get out.*"

The woman who ran the quaint bakery down the street was another story, however.

Vera had stopped at the last moment, seeing the pink storefront amid the dull rust brick of the surrounding buildings.

'VanLand's Bakery and Cafe' the sign read above the door in hand-painted swirled lettering.

"Morning!" said the woman behind the counter, greeting Vera cheerily from behind the counter, "What can I help you with?"

"How's the coffee?" Vera asked. She needed the caffeine to finish her drive, she was exhausted.

"Hot and fresh." the woman had said, gesturing for Vera to sit at a table near the door.

She poured a mug and delivered it to Vera, sliding it across the table, turning her head in complete curiosity at the stranger that invaded her bakery.

"Just passing through?" she asked Vera

Vera nodded. She didn't much feel like conversation, but she could see that the woman was desperate for it, "Yeah, I'm headed for the national forest."

"Ottawa?"

"That would be the one." Vera said. The coffee *was* hot and fresh, but the taste was lacking. She added two sugar packets to it and stirred, the spoon clanking awkwardly against the side of the mug, "Going to do some camping and hiking."

"Isn't it funny that people from the city escape to nature for their vacations, and people in the country like to visit the city for theirs?" the woman asked, hand on her hip, "I think everyone needs a change of scenery every now and then."

The look in her eyes reminded Vera of women in movies that dreamed of making it big in Hollywood.

"You got anything good on that menu?" Vera asked and pointed at the one that was still tucked under the woman's arm.

"Oh, sorry!" the woman said, her face slowly turning a shade of pink, "I'd forget my head if it wasn't attached. I would recommend the chicken salad, I made it myself. My husband says it's his favorite and it's one of my best sellers."

"Chicken salad it is!" Vera said and smiled. The woman was friendly, but had that small town romanticism about her. You could see the hope in her eyes, but you could also see the knowledge that she would never leave this town.

The chicken salad *had* been excellent and so was the chocolate donut that followed it. Homemade and still warm from the oven was the best way to eat a donut, Vera thought.

"Have you ever been out there?" Vera asked the woman, she still hadn't caught her name, "to the forest?"

"I went with my family a few times as a kid, but we stopped going after a while." the woman said, looking everywhere but at Vera, who found the way she had answered odd.

"Yeah?" Vera asked, "Anything in particular that stopped you from going back? Not to pry or anything."

The woman hesitated.

"Sorry, it's none of my business," Vera said, hands raised as if to say 'you don't have to answer that"

"No, it's okay." the woman said, "It's just been years since I've talked about it and it's one of those things that still feels fresh every time that I do, y'know?"

Nobody had entered the bakery since Vera had arrived, and it looked as though she may be the only customer that woman would have all morning. She didn't think they needed to worry about being interrupted any time soon.

"My family and I used to go camping there a lot when we, my brother George and myself, were kids. We had a lot of good memories there, swimming, kayaking, my dad taught us to fish there, even." she went on, smiling at the memories, "One night, in the summer of '86, we were camping with my dad along one of the unnamed streams that run through the forest. There had been a lot of rain that week before we went, and the water was going pretty fast, lots of flooded areas around. George wandered off to get some firewood like he had done a thousand times before."

Vera listened silently, now regretting having asked the question.

"They say that he fell into the stream and that his body was carried away," she continued with a sad smile, "He never cried out or anything like that. He was there one second and gone the next. We never found his body. It happens sometimes, especially in places like that. Too many dark corners hidden in plain sight. You'd be surprised how many people go missing in national forests and are never found."

"I'm sorry for bringing it up." Vera said. She was.

"It was a long time ago," she responded, but Vera could hear the shakiness of her voice, "we never went back after that. I remember being so upset with my parents about it, too."

"You wanted to go back?" asked Vera.

"I was only nine years old," she nodded, "and didn't understand what was going on. All I knew was that my brother was out there somewhere and I wanted to find him. It's the not knowing that's the worst in situations like that. You always hold hope."

"I'm sorry about your brother." Vera said, and took the woman's hand gently.

"Me too," she said, wiping away tears. Vera hadn't noticed that she had started crying, "He was a good kid. He was a year older and always my protector. He would have been a great man. You be careful out there."

Vera thought about what the woman had said as she drove the hilly terrain with rollercoaster-like dips and weaves. *"Too many dark corners hidden in plain sight."*

Just like the woman who had plunged over the side of the Mackinaw Bridge in her Yugo and hadn't been discovered for decades, thought Vera. Thousands of people passed over her grave every day for years and were none the wiser. Vera shivered.

Ottawa National Forest loomed ahead of her in the distance. It was a beautiful emerald green ribbon stretching for miles across the horizon, a river of leaves that hid a secret world.

She tried to keep the thoughts of last night's ugly business out of her mind and succeeded for the most part, except when an old Chevy truck had rolled up behind her to pass. She was sure it was going to be the two men, Errol and Davey, tracking her down. The truck pulled alongside her and an elderly man was at the wheel, frowning with concentration.

Four hours after leaving the rest area she finally arrived at her destination, and her main reason for making this trip. She shook with anxiety and excitement as she wound her way through the hardpan dirt roads, the trees towering far above her Jeep, great monoliths of a world that was.

Several families occupied the surrounding campsites.She was relieved. The solace of the U.P. was nice, but after last night and hearing the story about George today, she felt it safer to stick with a more populated area for the time being while she worked up the nerve to go it alone again.

She had to sort the pieces of her tent out before she could set it up. They had rattled around the floorboard and backseat the entire day after being so haphazardly tossed inside. She was missing at least one stake, but she made do with a well placed pine branch in its place.

She watched, not without envy, as families laughed together around their tent, or played frisbee with each other. The kids were forced to participate because their cell phones didn't have service, so they were mentally present. She thought of little

George, his little body somewhere still out in the forest she was about to embark in. The thought stung at her and frightened her.

"It happens sometimes, especially in places like that."

She wished desperately that she had gotten the chance to be a mother, and she had probably dodged a bullet by not having a child with Craig, but the longing was still there. She didn't know what kind of father Craig would have been, but after what had happened with the divorce, she didn't have high hopes for him.

"They say that he fell into the stream and that his body was carried away."

She shook the thought away violently and lit a cigarette, relishing the sensation of it burning her throat.

She smiled at a little girl of about seven years old that trolled by on her bicycle, training wheels stuttering against the ground jaggedly, and not helping much by the look of things. The girl waved happily and returned the smile, two front teeth missing and her tongue pressed through the gap.

"Are you having fun?" Vera asked her.

The girl nodded, "Yeah, we saw a bear!"

"Really?" Vera asked, dramatizing the excitement.

"Yeah, but it was in a cage. There was deer too, though." the girl said, looking down as if ashamed the bear had been caged, "but we see deer all the time."

"Tara," said the girl's mother as she approached from two campsites over, "What did we tell you about talking to strangers!"

"Don't?" Tara said knowingly, the same look on her face as when she had mentioned the caged bear.

"Sorry," Vera said, rising from the table she had been sitting at, "it was my fault, really."

The woman waved her hand, brushing the apology away as if it weren't needed, "We're just trying to teach her young. You never know people these days, I didn't mean any offence."

"None taken," Vera said, "You guys have a good night!"

"You too." The woman said, prodding her daughter along towards their temporary home.

Vera heard the coughing of the truck engine as it rolled slowly around the corner at the entrance of the campground.

"*It can't be.*" she thought aloud.

She couldn't be sure, it had been too dark to tell what color the truck the two meth cooks had been, but it sounded and looked similar enough that it caught her attention. It was an old box style Chevy with great wounds of rust on the back quarter panel.

She squinted through the darkness, trying to catch a glimpse of the occupants, who were only silhouettes against the fading sun. No luck. Even if it was them, would they recognize her? That had been dozens of miles away from here and the chances were miniscule.

"You're being paranoid, Vera." she said to herself as she climbed into the tent and burrowed deep in the sleeping bag.

The screaming started around eleven, prying Vera out of a dead sleep. She'd dozed off almost immediately after laying her head upon the pillow and dreamed horrible dreams of having to get firewood for her campsite and being trapped beneath the rushing waters of an unnamed stream, then watching as her family searched for her but never finding her.

Outside it sounded as though a gathering of women were wailing horrible, heart wrenching shrieks, like they had all lost their children in one fell swoop. The screams would come from one direction, then the other, creating a chorus of nightmarish conversation. She could hear the children at the other campsites asking their parents what the sound was. One of them had begun crying.

She felt for the gun that had been tucked under the pillow, found it, racked it. She listened closely, trying to focus on the sound, trying to identify the source. After

several moments she heard a couple
independent yips and barks, followed by a
skin-crawling howl.

" Coyotes." she heard someone say to one
of their children.

She sighed relief and wiped the sweat from
her tired brow. While they were loud and
fearsome sounding, these were an animal
that she experienced back home, though not
in the numbers in which they existed here.
They were typically harmless to humans,
cowardly at times, but would attack pets and
other small animals ferociously given the
chance. A pack could take down a deer if the
conditions were right. She lived near them
her whole life and only saw her first one just

last year when she hit it as it was crossing the road.

She lay in the dark for a long while listening to the sound of the ki-yi-ing. Coyotes were a vermin animal, but you had to admire their adaptation skills. Hunters had tried to send them the way of the gray wolf in the 1800s, killing them in the thousands. The coyote had prevailed, expanding its territory further than it had been before the government had launched their assault on them. While they had began in the American Southwest, they now infested every state, save for Hawaii. Hell, they even lived in the inner cities now. The creature moved further into the distance and she once again drifted into slumber. She had no dreams.

She woke early enough to watch the sun rise through the trees, it's warm glow illuminating the foliage in bright greens, dancing it's way through the canopy to warm her. She built a small fire just long enough to warm a pot of instant coffee and cook some bacon that she picked up at a small market on the trip yesterday. She sipped and ate greedily, the world coming alive around her, the birds lighting from their nests and the squirrels beginning their busy work of hoarding away nuts for the coming seasons.

She saw a garter snake slither it's way along the dirt path that wound through the campsites, a burst of color atop the packed brown dirt that disappeared into the tall grass.

She packed the tent into her hiking pack, taking care not to put the collapsible poles into any precarious angle where they could be broken. Packed beneath it were twelve MRE's, a gallon jug of water, the flare gun, a raincoat (just in case), first aid kit, and a small hatchet. Tied atop of it was her tightly rolled sleeping bag. As an afterthought she dropped the sheathed Ka-Bar into her left boot for good luck. She had seen her father carry it this way for many years. Her camera hung around her neck, swaying with every step forward. The Smith & Wesson rubbed angrily at her right thigh until she tightened the straps of the kydex holster, lessening the irritation.

The trees stretched to the sky, fingers of green grasping at the sun as the few fallen leaves from the previous autumn sang their dry snaps beneath her boots. The forest was laced with brooks and streams burbling into the steady thrum of a river as she pushed deeper.

Two black squirrels fought each other over the possession of an old arthritic oak, chittering with flicks of their bushy tails painting the air behind them. She snapped several pictures of the intense battle before telling them to break it up, sending them skittering for cover.

The sun boiled in the sky and the sweat stung harshly at her eyes. Two hours of hiking in the summer heat had taken its toll and she drank from the gallon of water she had along until she had to gasp for air. Her legs ached in pleasure and she rubbed them happily, resting long enough to catch her excited breath.

Her mother had tried telling her about the beauty here but she never expected the painted world that she was seeing before her. She was in the land of Oz, or Narnia, or any one of those fairy tale realms, but this was REAL and tangible in it's mystique.

In the distance stood a sheer rock face, trees perched atop it precariously, roots exposed as they grew outward from the edge and dangled.

"There." she thought, *"That is where I'm going to stay tonight."*

The trail faded off to the west as she headed southwest through the trees, stumbling over roots and fallen limbs. The cliff looked to be about five miles away, which would have taken no time at all using the trail, but wandering through the untamed lands slowed her down.

Teeth-like thorns tore at her jeans and arms as she wound her way through the undergrowth in the direction of the cliff, drawing small stinging tattoos of red. She would deal with them later when she had made camp.

The forest had become a tangled web that was impenetrable in places, so thick that it blocked out the sun, creating dark caves of brambles and ferns. Several times she heard the crashing of animals taking flight from her intrusion and she caught sight of deer and rabbits fleeing to safety.

"At least it wasn't a bear or a mountain lion."

She didn't want to overexert herself on her first day of hiking, but figured that she could get take a painkiller from her first-aid kit if warranted, and if that didn't help a little whiskey from her pocket flask would.

It took longer than expected to reach the base of the dark slate cliff face, three hours total, but upon reaching it she had no regrets. You could see how the wind had carved it over time, smooth in places from the water that surely would rage down it's crevice filled flank when the rain came. Littering the ground at its feet were boulders and large chunks of the slate that had broken off in millennia of erosion.

She snapped several pictures before setting the timer on her camera and running to the base of the cliff for a picture with the stunning backdrop. She would frame it as a gift for her mother's upcoming birthday.

After setting up base camp and suspending her food fifteen feet above the forest floor with a piece of paracord- it came with the new hiking pack- to keep away any critters, she explored her surroundings.

Set low on the cliff face she found a small cave approximately four feet wide and fifteen feet deep. She had to crouch to enter and dared not venture much further than the light would reach. The air was much cooler inside the cave, insulated by the thousands of tons of rock that surrounded it. It felt like the throat of a giant beast that could- at any moment- gobble her up whole. The thought hadn't occurred to her that a bear could easily be sleeping within, hidden in the dark recesses.

A falcon screamed and dove downward at dizzying speeds, plucking some kind of rodent from the clearing at the base of the rock formation and swooped upward in graceful fluid motion. To the west of where her tent lay, she found a brook that trickled softly into a small basin, the water so clear that it was hard to tell how deep it truly was.

"Only one way to find out." she shrugged to herself.

She stripped down to bare skin and jumped.

She gasped just before her head plunged below the previously placid water. Although the summer had been exceptionally warm and the sun shone high, the liquid was frigid, tightening her skin into hard pebbles.

The basin was only five feet deep and fifty feet around, just shallow enough for her head to poke out of it. She could feel no current and assumed that this was one of the tributaries that led into the larger streams and rivers.

"They say that he fell into the stream and that his body was carried away."

"Poor George," she said, splashing away a water bug that had come too close. It tipped, submerged, and then righted itself in the small ripples that probably looked like incoming tsunamis to the insect.

Unable to locate a way to ascend the monolithic stone, she thought she would try her hand tomorrow at hiking further along the base, hoping that it would slope gradually to a place where she could gain easier access. Rock climbing was not on her list of things she planned on trying during this adventure.

She found plenty of fallen limbs and twigs for a small fire, cutting them to a more suitable burning size with the hatchet. She brushed away any leaves or dry grass that could catch the flame and made a containment ring from the shattered remains at the bottom of the cliff. She would wait for sunset before lighting the fire, but felt it was better to be prepared than to stumble blindly through unknown terrain.

She checked her cell and was not shocked to find that service was nonexistent. She had planned on calling her parents, but forgot in the excitement of beginning the real adventure she had set out upon. The rest of the trip had just been the appetizer before this main course of week-long solidarity.

The biggest snake that Vera had ever seen lay basking in the sun near the basin she had jumped into. She cringed at the thought of jumping unknowingly onto such a creature, nearly five feet long and jet black, the underside of it's head a brilliant orange-red. She snapped a picture from a distance but dared not venture closer. It wasn't of the venomous variety, she didn't feel like tangoing with it.

"*Just be cool.*" she thought at it as she made a wide path around it. It watched her for a moment and then slithered slowly across the rocky landscape, it's muscles twitching it along lazily. She lost sight of it under one of the bigger boulders.

The trees that hugged the small clearing were ancient oaks that had trails of ivy and vines growing unabated up their twisted flanks. They had escaped the logging boom of the previous century, quietly living their near-immortal lives in serenity.

She napped before dining on a biscuits and gravy MRE that was surprisingly good. She had expected hospital cafeteria style food, but thought it was actually an improvement upon that concept. She had spent a week in the hospital as a kid and would never forget the hard-as-a-rock biscuit that she would swear had chipped her tooth. She had refused to eat another bite of anything they had brought. Even after the instruction to not bring anymore horrible meals they had, still charging them for it. She could still remember her dad absolutely losing his shit over that. She snorted a laugh at the memory.

Looking into the sky here was different than home; every star, every satellite that blinked through the vacuum of space, every shooting star. There were no lights to wash out the vastness of the universe.

The coyotes howled again as she lay down to sleep, she found them reassuring because they reminded her of home. Sleep took her quickly.

She heard the rain pitter-pattering at the fabric of the tent, running long shadowy veins down it in ominous shadows.

"*Shit.*"

Not a great way to start the day, but Mother Nature bows to no man (or woman for that matter). The tent was packed quickly, she would have to let it dry when the weather allowed, but it would still be sleepable. A little dampness never hurt anyone besides asthmatics and she was not one those unfortunate souls.

Following the face of the cliff westward was easier said than done as the slope became slick with mud and the smoothness of the bedrock that showed through in places. She nearly fell twice and then did the third time that her boot slid from beneath her, scuffing her knee into a bruise but otherwise leaving her unharmed.

"Sticks and stones can break my bones." she said aloud to herself, laughing as she was forced to scuffle down a particularly steep incline and into the treeline below. She would regain the slope later when it wasn't as taxingly steep.

The rain slicked the vinyl coat she had stowed away just for this purpose. The sound of splashing echoed against the now grass covered slope leading to the pinnacle of the rock formation and she followed them through the trees that brushed the beginning of the incline, coming to a small, grassy riverbank.

"I got one!" The boy said, his face lit up and wide eyed, fish at the end of his pole.

His father was just as excited and was beaming with pride."Great job, buddy! Let's reel it in!"

Vera observed the beautiful moment between the pair silently; a sharp pang of jealousy churned in her stomach. Life had taken a different path for her. Watching the exchange was a mixed bag of complicated emotions. She would likely never have this moment with a child of her own.

"Alright, here's the big catch! Let's get your picture with this big guy!" his dad said as he handed the fish to his son and grabbed the camera.

The boys could only stay still for three clicks of the camera, shaking with excitement. His eyes met with Vera's. "Did you see my fish? I caught it by myself!"

Vera smiled "I think that is the best looking fish that I have ever seen!"

His father spun around, hand involuntarily clutching at his chest, "Hello, I didn't see you standing there."

Vera apologized , "I didn't want to interrupt. I was just passing by and heard some of the excitement."

"You're not interrupting at all, we just don't often see people in these parts" replied his dad, "I think this one might be a little too small to keep, Jon." He measured the fish, shook his head and his son sadly toss the trout back, bottom lip extended in the way that only children can master. "Maybe the next one, bud."

Vera smiled as the little boy came running her way, over the loss of his big catch already, "We're gonna make smores!! Dad, Can she make smores with us?Please?"

His dad laughed, "I'm sure this nice lady has lots to do today, but she is more than welcome to make smore if she would like to stop and rest."

Vera crouched to meet Jon's eye level, "I would actually love a smore, they're one of my favorite snacks!"

She followed them further down the river bank where they had imitated her rock ring to contain the fire.   The man struck a match and dropped it on the bundle of sticks and dry grass that lay within, fanning it from a smoldering pile to a small blaze within minutes.

"Didn't happen to catch your name," the man groaning as he stood. He was handsome in the boy-next-door way; the dark swept back hair, solid build, great smile. He Looked to be in his late twenties to early thirties.

"Vera." she said, meeting his extended hand with enthusiasm, "And you are?"

"Craig," he said, "and this is Jon."

He must have seen the blood drain from her face because he looked concerned, "Are you okay, do you need to sit down?"

"Yeah, I'm fine," she said forcing a painted smile, "Just a little vertigo for a second or something."

The curious look he gave her clearly said that he didn't buy that story for one second, but he didn't press the issue any further.

"Dad!" said Jon, hands on his hips, "S'mores!"

They were on vacation from Green Bay, Craig told her as they roasted the marshmallows on broken twigs. The divorce was finalized in the spring and it was their first vacation with just the two of them. Jon was too busy trying to lick all the chocolate from his messy fingers to notice their conversation, humming contentedly to himself, legs swinging from the foldable chair in little happy kicks.

Vera paraphrased her own tale of love lost, leaving out the specifics. No need to clue in strangers on the fucked up tale that was her life.

"Dad, I want to catch a bigger one!" Jon had grown tired of grooming his fingers in cat-like fashion it seemed.

"Alright, bud!" Craig said, slapping his knees and rising with another grunt, and to Vera "Where you headed?"

She shrugged and gestured westward, "Out there."

"You be safe out there," he said, and leaned in closer with mock confidentiality, "There's lions and tigers and bears."

"Oh my!" Vera laughed. He *was* charming.

"Wait, there aren't tigers here are there?" It was Jon, an unsure inquisitive look scrunched upon his face.

"No, but there are wolves and those are just as bad!" his dad said, tossing his son's hair into a small tangled mess.

"I haven't seen any of those yet, though," Vera said, "so don't worry about them."

Jon looked only marginally more reassured.

"There's a pack out here somewhere that the Department of Natural Resources are tracking, but all we've heard this week are coyotes." said Craig,

"I heard them last night, sounds like there are quite a few." She said.

"Too many, that's for sure." he nodded, "It's been nice chatting with you, but I should get this monster back out fishing before we head back to the campground. It's supposed to storm pretty good tomorrow, so be prepared for that."

"I will, thanks." Vera said, shaking his hand. *"Maybe not all Craigs are bad."* She thought as she thanked them for the s'mores and wished them luck on the remainder of their fishing expedition.

The boy's smiling face was on her mind as she entered the grove of pines that sat midway up the incline.

"They say that he fell into the stream and that his body was carried away."

It was steeper than hell, but manageable, even if she did scuff the same knee she had earlier when she again lost her footing on a particularly slippery piece of the bedrock.

"Son of a bitch!" she rubbed at it. *"Sticks and particularly fucking stones."* she thought, not without a silent laugh.

She used the the trees for leverage, sometimes leaning against one at a precarious angle to catch her breath. The rain was now almost slowed to a stop and she she secretly hoped that the man had been wrong about strong storms moving into the area. The last thing she needed as a damned tree collapsing on her tent and crushing her like a bug.

The effort of climbing became easier after forty-five minutes of rugged hell; either the incline was plateauing or she was beginning to lose feeling in her legs. She assumed the former and prayed it wasn't the latter.

The view was spectacular. the rain had let up just enough to let the sun peak through the clouds. The early afternoon light dazzled the green tree-tops in every direction, and she saw soft glints and camera flashes of the reflecting rivers and streams that littered the paradise she had stumbled upon.

"*Holy shit.*" she said to herself in a whisper, her teeth widening in a piano key smile.

If there was a heaven, she thought it might be like this.

The sun had retreated quickly, as if it had appeared as a statement from Mother Nature, *"Gaze upon my creation in all its glory"*

Dinner was a pulled pork MRE and fresh blueberries that she found hidden along the ridge nestled above where she'd slept the night before. She desperately wished to peer over the edge, but feared the slickness of the rocks jutting upward into the sky would send her careening to her death.

"It's not the fall that kills you, it's the sudden stop." said her father's voice within her mind. That had always been one of his catchphrases, usually after hearing about a tragedy from height of any kind.

Crawling to the summit was the best option, she made the sacrifice willingly, soaking her knees against the sharp brittle rocks that cut like daggers and gouged at her stomach. Peering over the edge gave her an authentic case of vertigo, the dizzying height rolled her stomach like a bowling ball down a polished lane. The basin below looked less impressive from this perspective, almost like a puddle on a porch step.

The dark atop the cliff was heavier, like a weighted blanket putting claustrophobic pressure on everything it touched. Even the fire was not immune to its forces, it seemed to struggle with keeping lit. It was probably from the rain but Vera wouldn't rule out the impermeable blackness- that crept just at the edge of her camp- out as the culprit.

The coyote howls had ceased an hour ago, dinner had been apparently been particularly appetizing because the howls and yips reached a fever pitch that she never before experienced, it sounded as though they slunk around her campsite in rabid excitement, but knew they were hundreds of yards away. Sound carried up strangely at the summit. The only critter that *had* stumbled across her was a fat possum that hissed angrily as it passed.

"Hey, go fuck yourself, you long-nosed, cross eyed bitch." Vera said at it's departing back as it waddled awkwardly toward the treeline below.

The rain had not returned and she saw glimpses of stars between clouds that broke apart as they shape-shifted in the night like vaporious werewolves that disappeared into a misty swath of black sky. Orion the hunter stood watch over the universe, bow at the ready to slay the mighty Ursa Major, the big bear.

"Hopefully the bears stay far away from here," said Vera, sipping from the flask. She drank more tonight than she should have, "I don't need that kind of shit in my life right now."

If it hadn't been for Craig's bat-shit crazy antics, it's completely feasible that she would be a happy mother by now, doting upon the baby that looked far too much like it's father. Cooing and grabbing at her hair as it lay in her arm, eyes wide in curious wonder at the massive world it was struggling to understand.

She wouldn't be drinking whiskey in the dark at the top of a cliff, that's for sure.

"Fucking asshole." she said into the darkness, which seemed to bat the words back at her like a major league player, the echo calling out three times before fading.

The howl that shattered the calm was long and drawn out. The deep cry came from below and into the distance. There were no yips or ki-yi's that followed, but another howl, this one louder than the first and lasting so long that Vera wondered if it would. Those howl's said something that even a human such as Vera could translate: "We are here, we are hungry, this is our territory. We are wolves."

Her hand instinctively felt at her hip and she found the Smith & Wesson slumbering there, hoping she wouldn't have to wake it from it's slumber.

The light taps that played an off rhythm shuffle at the peak of the tent let her know that the rain had returned the next morning. Her head felt two sizes too big and her stomach had stormy seas of bile, which she vomited from the tent and onto the gray-wet bedrock.

"Never drinking again" she said. She took an aspirin from the first aid kit and chewed it, the bitterness giving her stomach another shift, but she managed not to vomit again.

She let the aspirin do it's work before deconstructing the tent heading west along the ridge, she felt like she was walking the back of a great, sleeping, stone snake.

"Snakes can strike." she thought, and moved further from the edge.

She was determined to make miles today, storm or no storm. She hiked for hours, her calves and thighs burning angrily at her. She walked through lunch- granola bar crunch- and was feeling considerably better than she had upon waking.

"Thank god for aspirin."

The storm hit around dinner time, preceded by winds of sixty-plus miles per hour. The rain stung at her and the branches above rattled like bucks battling in rut, always threatening to fall and skewer her through. She could see the low clouds that the winds pushed ahead of the storm, gray walls of smooth destruction that rolled ominously forward.

When the lightning began flashing closer and closer, as if it were a predator scenting it's prey, she relented and assembled her tent. The ferocity of the wind threatened to snatch it from her grasp but she moved behind the shelter of a huge sycamore which broke the gale enough to manage.

She prayed that the ancient tree could withstand at least this one last storm, she could be crushed in just the tick of the clock if it's roots gave out, or if one of the massive limbs plummeted from the sky.

Vera cringed at every strong burst of wind, waiting for it to die down. The way the storm tore at the sky, she was just hoping that a tornado didn't spin itself into existence and bear down upon her meek shelter, it would offer no protection from the debris.

The wind and rain relented after two hours, giving her just enough daylight to hike before the darkness became complete.

When she peaked her head from her tent, she saw that no limbs had been broken from the sycamore, but several pines along the ridge had been slain by the miniature derecho, he twisted limbs mangled under the weight of the trunk and the tall grass laid flat against the rocky ground beneath.

"That could have gone badly." she thought as she finished loading the tent onto her pack. She'd grown accustomed to the weight, though it still pulled at the muscles of her lower back, which by now were sore.

She made good time in the last remaining hours of light, the downward momentum of the slope pushing her along in staccato steps that lengthened as the angle declined. She estimated that she had made it four or five miles further into the wilderness and further from unannounced visitors and the likelihood of running into other wanderers.

"Sometimes you have to get lost to find yourself."

Trees lay strewn upon the ground throughout the forest, although she could not be sure it was from the storm that had just passed through or another offender. Some were pulled from the ground by the roots leaving deep pits that Vera imagined monstrous creatures dwelled within, and likely one day would in the form of coyotes or wolves, possibly a bear. Anything seemed possible in that darkness.

"Lions, and tigers, and bears" she thought as she climbed over the corpse of a humongous elm in her path.

"Oh my!" she said aloud and laughed heartily as she leapt from the fallen trunk.

She was still laughing when the jagged iron jaws of the bear trap slammed shut, shattering her right ankle and digging it's hungry teeth into the muscle. Her body collapsed as if falling victim to a controlled demolition and screams tore at her throat, threatening to rupture her vocal chords with their ferocity. Clutching at her ankle, the teeth of the trap unrelenting in its grasp. She dug frantically at the trap, trying to pry it open and free herself as blood began to leak around it's bite. It was a rabid dog bite of anger that she never before experienced.

"I am going to fucking die out here!" the voice in her head screamed as she fought to

remain conscious from the sheer shock of the attack. The pain was exquisite. Even the slightest movement caused it to radiate up her leg and down again, sharp and vicious.

Another calmer voice in her head spoke up. "*No. I will not die out here. I will not die wallowing in a goddamned bear trap just waiting to either die of exposure or be turned into bear shit. I am getting the fuck out of here!*"

She took off her belt, laying the holstered gun beside her, and tightening it as hard as she could just below the knee in a makeshift tourniquet to slow the bleeding, screaming as she did.

She wriggled free of her pack, gritting her teeth, feeling the metal scraping her broken bones as she shifted from side to side. She dug through it quickly and retrieved the hatchet. It was a sturdy piece of equipment, she made sure not to buy one of the cheap plastic-handled ones that would snap the first time you used it. She was especially thankful for that now.

 She dug the hatchet blade between the jaws of the trap and began prying as hard as she could. The trap began to open slowly as sweat poured from her in torrents. She put more weight into it and it opened more, she could feel the teeth slowly creeping out of her skin, until the hatchet slipped out at the trap and it once again slammed shut with a rusty thunderclap.

Vera's vision swam and she thought that she may actually faint from the new bout of pain that warranted another shriek of anger and torment. Sweat poured from her brow.

Pausing a moment to take several deep breaths before once again digging in the hatchet and prying at the opening of the trap.

Pushing with every fiber of her being, rage boiling her blood now and she ignored the pain, pushed through it, seeing the maw open inch by inch, feeling it grind against her bones as it released until, finally, she was able to wrench her ankle free of it and rolled screaming away from the contraption that had so grievously wounded her.

She cradled her broken ankle as she rolled to and fro on her back, her vision blinded by fresh tears of pain. She could feel the fresh flow of blood beginning to quicken around her fingers. The trap and her belt had stopped most of the bleeding but when the teeth had been removed it had found a clear route through. She pulled the belt tighter still.

She took off the light hoodie she had been wearing, and reached into her left boot, pulled the Ka-Bar from it's sheath. She cut several strips from the fabric and tied them tightly around the wounds, and then carefully replaced the knife. It didn't look as though the trap had punctured any major arteries, not for a lack of trying, but the damage was still gruesomely well done.

She lay on her back, the wet floor of the forest soaking her, staring up at the quickly darkening sky that peeked through the small openings between the trees. She could still hear the birds singing their happy songs as they flitted through the trees above, oblivious to her suffering below. Vera knew the direness of her situation. She was hours away from safety and would not be able to walk on her ankle. The trap had obliterated it and it hung sick and mangled from her leg. She thought of crawling but dragging the ankle behind her just made matters worse as it snagged and ragdolled in the dirt behind her, sending waves of pain shooting up her leg with the strength of a tsunami making landfall.

The pain was overwhelming in it's fury, as though a thousand wasps had descended upon her in great hoards, relentless in their bombardment. She only crawled a quarter of a mile in the last forty-five minutes, thankful that she at least had the Smith and Wesson to fend off any predators who may take her cries and the scent of blood as an invitation to dinner.

She cried out for help, hoping against all odds that there would be someone, ANYONE who may hear her. Maybe the man and his son would be within shouting distance. She didn't care if it was the antichrist himself ascended from hell, as long as somebody knew she was in this purgatory.

The sun was nearly touching the horizon when she offered a prayer to the gods of wireless and checked the service on her cell. Her prayers had once again not been answered. The battery was also flashing red at seventeen percent. She had forgotten to charge it in the Jeep overnight; it slipped her mind because she hadn't been attached to it without the constant alerts buzzing in her pocket. She enjoyed the break from the constant barrage of information but now felt foolish for not treasuring the ease of contacting another human with the simple swipe of a button.

Nobody would be worried or think of reporting her missing to the authorities for at least a week, maybe longer. She could very well end up just another ghost of the national forest system. It could be years before anyone found her, if they found her at all.

" *It happens sometimes, especially in places like that.* "

She needed to get back to the campground, to the Jeep. There would be people there who could help her, get her to the hospital. She began to cry silently as she drug herself onward, hopping on one knee and dragging the other, through a wall of thickets that gouged and tore like the talons of angry hawks at her exposed arms.

She crawled at a painfully slow pace trying to be delicate. If she could find a long enough branch that she could crutch herself along much faster. She had her first stroke of luck since her maiming and found one that was long enough and supported her full weight at the base of an oak.

The makeshift crutch did speed things along but not by much. It dug probingly into her armpit as she pushed her weight into it, trying to keep her foot from touching the ground and snagging. Vera nearly fell several times as the weight of her pack shifted, throwing her off balance. She thought if she could keep this momentum she might be able to make it back to the camp within 6 hours. She would have to brave the abyss through the blanket of night that would soon be covering the land.

She could hear an owl in the distance asking querying it's eternal question and the crickets sang in ferver at a near deafening volume. Several snakes slithered off through the brush as she approached; short, fat thick ones that ribboned away at a speed faster than Vera could have walked on a day when she wasn't minus a useful appendage.

She propped herself against the base of a large tree, it's bark smooth to the touch and cooling on her sweat-drenched skin and watched as the sun kissed the horizon, sinking through the quicksand of sky that swallowed it whole.

Part Two

The Levee Breaks

Chapter One

Fred Hardwick never liked Craig. He kept his judgment to himself and had not shared it with either Vera or Moira. He he long ago resigned himself to the fact that his opinion never seemed to do anything besides complicate the situation more than just shutting the hell up did.

The little bastard had proposed and Vera had accepted. When she asked Fred what he thought, he had given her the stock answer that he learned kept the peace in his world.

"You know what is best for you, Kiddo."

He remembered Vera hugging him tightly, "Thanks, Daddy."

He deeply regretted not telling her to boot his ass to the curb the first night she had introduced him to them.. He just sensed something off about Craig. He was a small, weasel of a man that both Vera and Moira fawned over. He was good looking, but from where Fred stood, good looks were no substitute for moral fiber.

He knew that he couldn't change the past and now had to deal with the present situation: a daughter grieving a divorce from a man that had tried to murder both her and her family in drunken rage.

Fred had been pissed when Moira brought
up her backpacking trip across the Upper
Peninsula. She lauded that trip as being life
changing and transcendental to Vera, but
Fred remembered Moira coming home
complaining about how badly the
mosquitoes had bitten her and how
miserable she had been without access to her
usual amenities.

He confronted Moira about this the night
she had suggested the trip to Vera. He
waited until they were in the car and on the
road, of course. He knew there would be a
fight in his future, no crystal ball needed.

Moira reducing herself to tears the moment
Fred had reminded her of the true facts of
her life-changing journey.

"Well, what the hell did you want me to say to her, Fred?" Moira had said spitefully through her tears, "Sorry that your husband tried to fucking murder you and now you have to start over?"

Fred was used to these outbursts of Moira's, and usually avoided them by choosing his words carefully. This night had been different. Maybe he was just tired of Moira's fairytale spin on retrospect or maybe he had just woke up on the wrong side of the bed that morning.

"If you want to live in the land of make believe, Moira," he had said, "that is fine. What you will not do is fill our daughter's head with an idea that you couldn't hack. I think we remember your little trip very differently, because I had to be the one to come pick your sorry ass up from that shitty little diner on Highway 2 three weeks early, and you just sold the idea as if it were the most positive thing that has ever happened to you."

Moira said nothing the rest of the way home and Fred knew instinctively that he would be sleeping on the couch. He didn't even care at that point, he was disgusted that Moira had spun their daughter's grief into a fairytale about her own past instead of trying to address the situation head on. That's what Moira was best at these days, though: avoiding an ugly truth with a beautiful lie.

When Vera had at first shot down the idea of the solo trip up north, Fred had been able to breathe easy, but when she changed her mind after selling the house he told Moira to tell Vera the truth about the trip she had taken or he would do it himself.

He gave up on that ultimatum after seeing the way Vera prepared herself for the journey north. He always thought of her as her mother's child but maybe she had a little more of his genes in her than he had assumed. He could see the pride in her eyes when she showed him the supplies she had gotten and she thoroughly impressed him with her dedication to learning what she needed to know to survive up there. He thought that Vera could pull off what her mother failed at attempting, and he thought it would be good for her.

He always loved Vera, of course, but she had been a neurotic mess even in her teenage years. Maybe it was his fault for not putting his foot down and telling Moira to lay off the poor kid. She had berated Vera with "what-ifs" and "what-mights" the entirety of her life and by the time Vera had graduated high school Fred could already see that Vera would never be a risk taker in her life. She lived in fear of the judgment of Moira and that inhibited her from the adventure that all kids should be entitled to.

He insisted that Vera buy herself a handgun for the journey, the bigger the better. Moira had taken her turn at being pissed about the firearm but knew better than to bring it up. She didn't want to risk

Fred revealing her little secret. He also insisted on training her to use it himself. He had spent his entire life around guns and had carried them into combat.

Fred didn't like to talk about or even think about war any more than his brain would force him to. He had seen what horror that guns were capable of in the hands of the right person,. Charles Whitman, for example had been one of those people.

Fred knew he was better off than some of the others who had come home scrambled or poisoned, if only by the grace of God. He just had that uncanny ability to compartmentalize his tragedies.

Vera had become one with the gun almost immediately and surprised Fred with the tenacious precision which she commanded of the pistol in her hand. She couldn't out-shoot him just yet, but a few more months of practice and she would be nearing his now shaky spread.

He wasn't the spring chicken he had once been and although he would never let Vera see it, she had given him a run for his money when it came to setting up her tent. He had been winded and trying to get her to give up on it but they had continued well into the dark, until he had called it quits. Vera impressed her old man and he was happy to see her smiling as they deconstructed the tent for the last time.

"Thanks for helping me with all of this, Dad." she said and kissed him on the cheek.

He had been rendered stunned for a moment, it had been years since she kissed him on the cheek. That stopped about the time she brought home her first boyfriend, Aaron, whom Fred had liked much more than Craig. He never knew what happened with Vera and Aaron and it wasn't in his disposition to ask such things. Some things were better left unknown when it came to being a father.

Fred had spent more time with Vera the last month before her trip than they had spent together in years, which he had come to regret. He let life pass him by and his little girl had grown into quite the independent woman, even if she didn't know it yet.

Vera made him proud in the way that she so determinately set herself a goal and worked for it, following all of his advice and surpassed it in most ways. He felt this trip was a bad idea in the beginning, but if one woman in the family could legitimately pull this trip off, it would be Vera.

Fred spent a considerable amount of time in the U.P. as a child and later as an adult. His family once owned a cabin in the Copper Harbor area, which was about as far north as you could get before you were in Canadian waters.

He hunted black bear and moose there, winning the luck of the draw with the state lottery for permits. The populations were carefully regulated and you had to play the odds to win the ticket. He knew how rugged the terrain could be and especially how volatile the locals could be.

He had gotten into a bar room brawl as a twenty-something with a local over the simple argument of being from the Lower Peninsula and winning the bear tag. Yoopers didn't like the Trolls- those that lived south of the bridge- infringing on their sacred territory that they felt entitled to. They had beaten the hell out of each other and Fred still wasn't sure who bested who in that match, but he had one hell of a shiner for a week and a half after and likely a concussion to boot.

Fred could remember when his father demanded the phone company run a line to the cabin in case of emergency, which they had refused citing lack of resources. Instead of paying the phone company to install the poles and line, his father had done it himself, Fred and his uncles helping to cut down on cost. The phone company had been none too happy to miss out on that cash and threatened to not let them install the line. His father threatened to do that himself as well and the phone company finally caved.

It had been this landline on which Moira would call him to be rescued from a restaurant on Highway 2 several years later. They hadn't even been married at that point and Fred had been completely smitten with Moira. He jumped at the chance to play knight in shining armor.

They met in their hometown of Fenton, just south of Flint, Michigan. Fred had just come home from the war and was working for his father in his used car lot. He was terrible at the job and couldn't stand having his old man sign his paycheck every week, but it was a living.

Moira had been fresh out of college and came in with her father to buy herself her first car. Fred thought she was the prettiest girl he had ever laid eyes on as he half-heartedly tried to convince her to buy one of the beaters on the lot.

When he was sure they were out of earshot from any of the other salesmen, he recommended that they go Guiman's Used Cars just up Fenton road.

"They have better cars, honestly, and their warranty is second to none. I just don't want you to waste your hard earned money, here." He said.

Moira's father appreciated the honesty and shook his hand before they left, thanking him. It was by sheer happenstance that he would run into her again that very same Friday night at one of the very few drive-ins the state had left.

He hadn't wanted to go out at all but he had been talked into it by the only other salesman that he could stand, Jon Rob Tomlinson.

"Never John, Never Rob, always Jon Rob." was Jon Rob's go-to introductory line and Fred cringed every time he said it, whether it be to a customer or one of the girls who seemed to have an unnatural dislike for the two-named phenom.

They had gone to see some B Horror movie double feature, Fred couldn't remember which ones anymore, and Jon Rob had used his catchphrase on Moira in line at the concession stand.

She laughed but to Fred's surprised she had leaned passed Jon Rob and spoken directly to him.

"Here I was thinking you were a respectable handsome man and then I find you with this piece of work!" she said and winked.

"Hey, I'm giving you my best material here, lady!" Jon Rob laughed, clutching his heart in mock hurt.

"If that's your best material, I think you have some work to do, champ." Fred said, "Forgive him. He knows not what he does."

Fred felt his face grow warm and could see the roses blooming on Moira's face as well. It had been kismet, indeed. They shared their very first impromptu date that night, abandoning their respective parties to sit together on the swings at the base of the massive movie screens. Kids usually ran rampant on the swings, but with the horror double feature it seemed that they were nowhere in sight.

Moira had driven her newly purchased car, courtesy of Guiman's Used Cars and she offered him a ride home after finding that Jon Rob left him to fend for himself.

"Must be that someone fell for his smooth talking," Fred said, not actually believing that someone had. He had never actually seen it work and if he were to place bets he would do so on Jon Rob failing in his quest and going home with "Miss Michigan".

The ride home had been welcomed, it had started to drizzle as the credits played on the last movie, and Fred hadn't felt like walking home in the oncoming downpour.

He thanked her for the ride home and she responded with a kiss. They had gone steady from that moment onward and were married two years later. They tried for kids and had all but given up when Brenda came along. Vera showed up five years later unexpectedly.

Vera called nearly every day of her journey.

Fred had an idea that she knew he was apprehensive about her journey and wanted to quell an old man's fear. Moira had seemingly gotten over his moment of truth and told him to pick up the second line every time Vera had called so she could tell them both about her adventures in the Great North.

When the phone calls had stopped, Fred knew that Vera must have reached the western side of the U.P. That side was basically a dead zone until you got towards the Wisconsin side and more toward civilization, if you could call anything in Wisconsin civilization that is.

He expected the calls to stop as she ventured out on her own and while he was nervous, he was also excited for her. He truly hoped that she could do what her mother couldn't and it might finally shut Moira up about her fantasy trip when her daughter had experienced the real thing. He had his doubts about that, however.

This had been the first night that Vera hadn't called and Fred was uneasy. He knew that service was nonexistent; he just had anxiety about the whole matter. If anything were to happen, nobody would be able to help her and hell, they weren't even sure where she was going to be on any given day. Vera wanted to fly by the seat of her pants, bouncing from place to place and he was sure she was doing exactly that.

"It's natural to worry, Dear!" Moira said, stroking his hair as she passed behind his reclined chair, "She will be fine."

"Until she's not." Fred said coldly. He hadn't meant for it to come out so harsh but it did all the same.

"Sorry, Moira," he sighed, "I think I'm just tired."

She forced a smile but Fred could see the hurt in her eyes. He beckoned her closer and kissed her hand. He did still love her, by god. She may drive him insane most of the time but he knew she meant well.

They went to bed together for the first time in weeks that night. As they lay there in silence, Fred hoped that Vera was having the adventure that she had been hoping for. Fred could not shake the anxiety that plagued him. Something didn't feel right and he didn't like it. Moira had reassured him that Vera was fine and was likely having the time of her life, but that growing doubt that churned in his stomach kept growing in its malignancy.

He would call the ranger station up there in the morning just in case. He wanted them to be on the lookout for her should anything have happened. If nothing else, they would know she was in the area. He made sure to mention her Wrangler and plate number.

"We'll keep an eye out while doing our rounds and let you know if we happen to bump into her, she most likely just doesn't have service on her phone!" the Ranger said. He had given his name as Torres and sounded genuine enough to Fred, "We have to use the SAT phones ourselves up here."

"I'd appreciate that. She's likely fine and I'm just an old man worrying." Fred said.

The call had settled Fred's nerves a bit. He knew he was overreacting, but it was better to be safe than sorry.

Moira scolded him for the call, "She's old enough to not need us helicoptering over her, Fred! She's a grown woman for Christ's sake!"

Moira was right, of course. Vera didn't need them hovering about and babysitting her every move, and he now felt embarrassed at having made the phone call.

He decided that going for a drive might clear his mind. Moira was suffocating in her constant harassment over the call to the ranger station.

He cruised westward on I-69, the top down on his Mustang, the wind jostling his gray hair about.

He hated himself for the contempt he now held for Moira. It hadn't always been this way. After the kids were born they settled down in a small but affluent home in Grand Blanc, an upscale neighborhood with low crime-rate and friendly neighbors.

He could remember the nights when he would put the girls to bed, reading them something from his own personal collection of books instead of the children's books lining the shelves of their room.

Moira would stand hidden just outside to doorway, listening. She thought he didn't know about that, but he could hear her quiet footsteps sneaking down the hall, wanting to hear the stories. He let her keep that secret.

Fred signaled north towards US-127. He didn't have a specific destination in mind. *"Sometimes you just have to get lost to find yourself again."* he thought, letting the speedometer creep past 80.

Things had changed when Fred found a career in analytics. The hours were longer, but the pay was infinitely better, plus benefits and insurance.

The adjustment had been jarring to Moira, who had grown used to the time they would spend together as a family. She didn't understand that he was sacrificing his time to build a better future for them.

"Is it because of me?" He could remember her asking one night when he hadn't come home until past midnight. Her eyes had been puffy in the way that only hours of crying seemed capable of doing. She suspected an affair, one that he was not having.

He reassured her as much as he could, but the argument had grown tiresome quickly and the fights grew more frequent. They even separated for several months- although the girls seemed to not remember this- and they never reminded them.

They reconciled when Vera came down with Scarlet Fever. Days and nights in the hospital, it was touch and go for awhile- her little body couldn't handle the fever that was cooking her from the inside out. The doctors packed her in a tub of ice at one point to lower it, and he could still remember her agonizing screams calling for their help, and them being unable to answer those cries.

Fred shook the thought from his head. It was like looking through the attic and finding a trunk-full of forgotten pictures. Sometimes you forget things, but every now and then they creep as if they had just happened with horrible, vivid detail.

"Just like the war." he said aloud to himself.

Those memories haunted his subconscious for years. He still couldn't fully enjoy fireworks on the 4th of July, and the gunfire on opening day of deer season did tend to set him on edge while he sat in his blind. He understood what some people said about houses not being haunted, it's the people.

He could still see the faces of his dead friends when he closed his eyes every night, and heard their voices in his dreams, asking why *he* was the one to survive and why *they* had died.

Moira never asked about any of it, and he never told. He thought she knew better, sometimes things are better left unsaid.

No. Moira did not want to know those things. She wanted to know how he felt or what he was thinking about at a superficial level. If she ever learned of the things that he had done, that he had been a part of, she would never look at him the same again. She never asked about the dreams that sometimes woke him in the night, screaming in their sweat-soaked bed. Those dreams were few and far in between now, but hadn't always been.

He punched the accelerator of the Mustang and flew further north away from the crowded bustle of cities and into farm country.

He stopped at an apple orchard that was adjacent to the highway. The sign claimed they had the best hard cider in the state, and he fully intended on throwing one back to wash away the self-created sorrows.

It was a definite tourist trap with all kinds of kitschy items and organic this and organic that. He was amused by the self-playing piano that drummed out an old tune that he recognized but couldn't quite place a name on. He thought it was something by Roy Clark.

The sign had been telling the truth, it was one of the best damn ciders that Fred ever tasted. He'd lost the taste for beer years ago and welcomed the sudden fad of craft brewed beverages with open arms. Not everything that the younger generations created was complete shit after all.

His cell rang, Moira's name displayed on the screen. He swiped right to answer the call.

"Hey." he said. He wasn't sure how this call would play out after the morning fight.

"I'm sorry." she said, her voice with a mouse-like timidity to it.

He was surprised. Moira didn't issue apologies easily, and especially didn't hand them out unprompted.

"It's okay, you were right." he said, taking a swig of the cider. It helped to wash down the taste of admitting she was right.

There was a moment of silence on the phone and Fred thought for a moment he might have lost service. He was about the check it when Moira finally spoke up.

"I don't know if either of us were right, Fred." she said, her voice breaking, "I don't know what happened to us. It just isn't the same anymore, is it?"

Fred considered this, "Maybe we just got old, babe."

She laughed, but Fred could tell she was crying,

"Yeah, we definitely did that. I don't even know when that happened."

"Hell if I know." Fred said and managed a smile in spite of himself.

"Will you be back tonight?" she asked.

Fred could hear the hopefulness in her voice.

"Yeah, I just had to get out," he said, "clear my head for a bit, y'know?"

"Did you get a speeding ticket in that thing?"

Fred laughed. Last summer he had gotten three of them and Moira kept threatening to sell the Mustang if he got another one in it, "No, no ticket. They could never catch me."

"Come home, please."

"I'll be there in about two hours." he said, finishing the bottle and dropping it into a metal recycling can. It was nearly full to the brim and swarming with bees after the sweet smells that emanated from within. He swatted away one that ventured too close to his face.

"I love you, Fred."

He hesitated, but only for a moment.

"I love you too, Moira."

He hung up. He decided to grab a six-pack of that cider before he left. Maybe they could drink some later.

He tossed the six-pack in the back seat and put the car in drive. He was looking forward to going home. Maybe they could have a long overdue and much needed talk.

Chapter Two

 The white light of the moon cascaded
downward in a welcomed offering from the
cosmos. Vera was thankful for any favor she
could get and the moon would provide at
least some guiding light through the wild
country that she still had to traverse.
Her stomach growled audibly in hunger. She
ate half of an MRE and drank her water
sparingly. She could maybe find another

spring or river to refill the bottle if she had to,

but she wasn't keen on the idea of drinking bacteria filled water, except as a last resort. She was already crippled and did not particularly want to give herself a stomach virus and weaken herself further. She could just imagine being curled into a ball and trying not to soil herself.

She actually laughed out loud at this in spite of her fear. She laughed uncontrollably until her ribs hurt and tears streamed down her face in rivers. It was no laughing matter but the image had struck her as funny and the laughter felt good to her. It felt like hope.

The sun had been her compass and with it's vanishing she no longer knew which direction she would be going. She could either risk stumbling deeper into the forest or wait until the sunrise. After weighing her options, she chose to find the best shelter she could, one which she could easily defend should a creature of the night scent her wounds and decide to investigate. The tent would be easy shredding for a predator.

She found a tree whose ancient top lay next to it. The base had rotted itself hollow and she could squeeze through the tight opening just enough to slide inside. She had to grit her teeth against the pain as she shifted her weight to her bad foot inorder to fit the rest of the way in.

It was snug inside and if it rained she would surely be at the mercy of the elements through the exposed top, but it did offer her some protection and she would take any she could get in this environment.

She found that if she shifted just right that she could sit, albeit uncomfortably, inside the tree's large base. Most of the bleeding from her ankle had stopped but the sharp stabbing pains were now accompanied by dull, pounding aches with every beat of her heart.

She pulled her pack through the opening in the tree, she had to free herself from it to fit through the gap. She wedged it between the two sides to keep out any smaller animals and felt much more at ease now that she wasn't quite as exposed. She chewed four aspirin from her kit.

The coyotes and their maddening cries broke the silence. They sounded close by and she sat guarded, pistol in hand should they make an appearance and try to trespass upon her claimed sanctuary. They moved into the distance after a time and she relaxed. Every nerve ending had been lit with electric anxiety for hours and she fought the urge to sleep.

She was exhausted in ways she could never imagine possible and her ankle was steadily growing more pained. She fought the urge to nod of into the land of dreams, catching her head as it dropped to her chest several times.

The tree seemed more spacious when she had first crawled inside but now her legs were cramped and the small of her back was stiff with the lack of mobility. She could almost hear it creaking, a rusted iron door in the dark.

A bobcat slunk through the forest, it's rippling muscles visible under the fur. It paused and looked in her direction but continued on when it decided that there was nothing of use to it. It was on a mission to find it's next tasty morsel, and full-grown human was far too large for it to consider as prey. It moved with the grace of a dancer through the forest silently and darted out of sight.

Were it not for her current condition, Vera would have tried to capture a photo of it. As things were, she watched in silent wonder at the forest coming alive around her.

The next wave of howls were the same she had heard the night before. Vera had no doubt that the wolves were out, possibly even hunting the coyotes (who had vacated the area, likely submitting the territory to the larger predator.)

The howls were close, much closer than they had been and Vera's blood ran cold when she heard the sound of leaves and brush being ruffled across the forest floor in whisping sounds, barely audible inside of the tree. Her heart raced, knowing that they could smell the trail of a wounded animal in the air, the trail she had left behind her.

She could feel the sweat building between her palm and the pistol as she went into high-alert.

The yips surrounded her and in the darkness she saw a large wolf appear in the one sliver of moonlight that shimmered through the canopy and kissed the fur of the canid in a glowing caress. She watched as it sniffed the air, it's head

turning slowly in her direction. She had raised the gun as quietly as she could and now had it pointed in it's direction.

The wolf threw its head back and let out a long, haunting howl to it's companions.

Vera knew instinctively what it meant: "I have found the wounded animal. I have found

dinner. Come and get it."

It stood about fifteen yards away, pacing. It was waiting for it's pack to arrive to increase the odds of taking down their prey. She saw the moon reflecting sharp beads of light from its eyes like white diamonds when it would turn from one direction to another. It's heavy breathing growing more excited in the anticipation.

Vera heard the footfalls of it's compatriots gathering in volume, eager for their meal.Her hands began to tremble, the gun a salt shaker in her hand.

The range had not prepared her for this. The motionless, black, silhouetted targets of faceless men were not comparable to the speed and agility of a wolf, let alone an entire pack.

Four of them appeared from the darkness, circling the one that had scented her out. It was clear to vera that it was the alpha that found her based on the way the others looked to it for their next move, their plan of attack. They chittered and whined in cacophony at one another, communicating like conspirators in an sinister plot.

Vera tried to steady her hands but the gun was an anvil and the barrel kept wanting to nod toward the ground. If they came any closer she would squeeze the trigger and hope for the best. She had been a fairly decent shot at the range, her father had showed her how to hold the gun,align the sights, to squeeze the trigger and not to pull it. What he hadn't prepared her for was to be shooting at multiple targets in the darkness when she had suffered a major trauma.

The alpha nipped at two of the others closest to it,
keeping them behind the line that it held. The alpha let out another howl and lowered its head, leading the charge directly at the tree in which Vera lay hiding.

She sat in silent terror, seeing the five creatures running in unison at her, hearing their heaving breaths panting in the darkness as they wound their way through the saplings in the small clearing.

Vera tried to steady her hands and outstretched her arms,
gun aimed. Her breath caught in her chest and her heartbeat pounded with the adrenaline surging throughout her body. She squeezed her hands tighter around the pistol grip and pulled the trigger.

The first shot had missed the charging wolves and Vera felt the dread set in as the grew closer by the second. Soon they would be upon her, their greedy mouths snapping at her through the gap in the tree. Her sanctuary could quickly become her tomb, there was no way out.

Vera looked down the barrel of the gun, the sights barely visible in the inkly black surrounding her, and pulled the trigger again.

This time one of the wolves yelped in pain and Vera saw it stumble and veer off from the rest. She hope she had killed the fucking thing but had no way of knowing for sure.

The sound of the pistol was deafening in the confines of the tree and she was reminded of Craig firing his own gun at Paul from his truck.

She could no longer hear the wolves padded feet tearing toward her. Instead it was replaced with a loud ringing which flooded out all other sounds.

She pulled the trigger again and this time saw one of the alpha's front legs give out as it slid snout first into the dirt and rolled several times before coming to a stop.

The rest of the pack all broke in different directions, having lost their leader. The alpha tried to gain it's footing, but she had hit it where the leg met the shoulder on the left side. She had been aiming for the head, but she would take what she could get at this point. It gave her enough time to carefully re-aim the pistol and fire another shot.

This one took most of the top of the wolf's head off. One of the ears had disappeared in a bloody mist. The beast's head dropped to the ground and it's legs stiffened in the death throes that wracked its body.

Over the ringing in her ears she could hear the rest of the pack howling. This was not the howl of an animal preparing for another attack, but the sound of family members mourning a loss of a loved one.

Vera sobbed loudly in the dark hole of the tree in which she sat. She had never willingly killed another living being and though it was in self-defense, she couldn't help but be filled with guilt. The animal had just been doing what it had been made to do and here she was to end it in the dark in such a terrible way for such a beautiful creature.

The howls grew louder as the wolves called to one another, sharing in their grief.

Vera cried with them until the land fell silent and she heard them no more.

She must have fallen asleep in the haunting silence because she startled at the sound of more yipping and barks. She raised the gun and prepared to fire, but saw that it was not the rest of the pack she had fended off.

Instead she found five coyotes gnawing at the remains of the alpha wolf. She heard them tearing at the flesh of the bigger predator, wet sloshing sounds that made her stomach cartwheel and she fought down the vomit that began to crawl slowly up her throat.

She considered shooting them but, not wanting to waste bullets, she had to live and let live. She didn't know if the wolves would come back and she didn't want to waste precious ammo on coyotes when she could just spook them, which she did by banging the hatchet against the tree and roaring as best she could. The vermin darted away into the darkness with cries of anger and confusion.

The night sky was giving way to a lighter shade of blue. The sun would soon peek out from its slumber and she could begin the arduous trek eastward to safety.

The pain in her ankle subsided in the night, she was sure that would change once she began limping her way through the labyrinth that lay ahead. The promise of daylight being so near had breathed new hope into her possibly surviving this nightmarish peril.

She shimmied from the hollow at first light, the birds already in full orchestration at the conducting prowess of the warmth beaming through the land.

Her ankle began throbbing in sharper bursts of pain as she crutched her way through the forest with the sun in her face. She paused briefly to examine the remains of the alpha wolf that had stalked her the night before.

It was a gray wolf, the bigger of the two breeds that populated Michigan- the other being the Eastern. It's fur was gorgeous, even through the blood that had seeped into the white, discoloring it in jarring contrast. The coyotes had torn at its hind end, and it's guts were strewn from the opening, flies already feasting. She could no longer hold in the vomit.

She had to squint to see clearly and longed for her Ray Bans that she had left sitting on the dash of her Wrangler. She also longed for medical attention and stronger painkillers, but the sunglasses would be a great start.

She crutched herself along for two hours- the process had gotten easier with experience- and she was moving at a fairly amiable pace. She stopped long enough to finish off the MRE from the day before, washing it down with swigs of water.

The blood coagulated in a crusted black and brown armor around her damaged ankle and- using the rest of her water- she rinsed the wounds as best she could. The bones had not penetrated the skin, but the peculiar angle at which it dangled was no less reassuring than if it had.

A bald eagle soared above on the thermals which radiated in waves from where the bedrock showed through the forest floor, harping screeches as it stalked for its prey.

She lumbered awkwardly eastward, tripping and nearly toppling over roots and fallen limbs every few seconds- this area of the forest was far more overgrown than where she had begun her journey and she couldn't help but fear that she was headed in the wrong direction, even with the sun

leading her march along the downward
slope.

　She cried out in happiness when she saw a
path ahead, just on the other side of some
thorn bushes, which she barely felt as she
pushed through them and fell crying into the
clear dirt path. She was safe.

Chapter Three

Fred tossed the six-pack in the back seat and put the car in drive. He was looking forward to going home. Maybe they could have a long overdue and much needed talk.

The phone rang again.

"Damn it, Moira," said Fred, putting the car back in park and fidgeting in the pocket of his jeans to retrieve the cell, but found that it was a number calling from Marquette.

"Hello? Vera?" Fred asked, relieved.

"Hello?" the voice sounded far away, "Is this Fred Hardwick?"

"Yes?"

"Sir," the voice said in an official sounding tone, "This is Officer Erickson with the Michigan State Police."

Fred's stomach dropped and his heart felt as though it had sank to where his stomach had been.

"We found your Jeep Wrangler wrapped around a tree on Highway 2 just south of Ottawa National Forest. Were you involved in an accident?"

The world seem to spin around Fred and he felt as though he may vomit. He felt sweat beading on his brow.

"No," he said quietly, struggling to find his breath. "It's my daughter's, I cosigned for it."

"Well," said Officer Erickson, "We're going to need you to come in, are you in the area?"

"Is she okay?" Fred asked, prepared for the worst.

"Sir, we only found the Jeep. There was some blood but not enough to mean a fatality. We need you to come in, please."

Fred called Moira to tell her about the Jeep before he slamming the accelerator to the floor and shooting north on US-127, leaving a cloud of dust and melted tire in the parking lot of the cider mill. She would meet him in

Marquette but would be several hours behind.

He hadn't given her the obligatory, "I told you that something was wrong."

He crossed the Mackinaw Bridge three and a half hours later, fighting the urge to keep the accelerator to the floor. The toll booths and police kept his speed at bay, but when he reached the highway he once again resumed his speed, a red streak down the highway in the fading sunlight.

He pulled into the state police post an hour and a half after crossing the bridge. He found Officer Erickson waiting for him behind a desk inside.

"Did you find her?" Fred inquired after introducing himself.

Erickson shook his head, "I'm sorry but no. It looks to us like the Jeep was stolen. The driver's side window is smashed and it was hotwired. Do you have any idea where she might have been?"

Fred's heart pounded. Stolen. They could have killed her and taken the Jeep for all he knew, her body lying somewhere in the thousands of acres of National Forest, impossible to find.

"No," he said, "we haven't heard from her in two days. We figured she'd lost service on her cell, but now I'm not so sure."

"We are sending the chopper out tomorrow for a search of the area near where we found the vehicle," said Erickson, "It's pretty thick forest out there though. We are trying to find enough men for a ground search but they have to fly up from down-state. I'm sure we'll find her."

Fred was not hopeful. He knew how searches went in the National Forest system. There were people that vanished without a trace, some that were found years later- miles from where they had disappeared- and some that were found either mauled to death by animals, exposure, or murdered. There was even that bastard out in Yosemite that ended up being a serial killer a few years back, picking off visitors of the park.

Fred had gotten a room at an old motel along the highway after leaving the station. He cried then, alone in the room before

Moira arrived four hours later. She burst into tears when she saw him, throwing her arms around him.

"What happened?" she asked, wiping away her tears when they separated. He told her what Erickson told him.

"Oh my god." she sighed, "What are we going to do?"

"We'll go out looking. Give me your keys, I'm driving the truck." he said.

They tore down highway until they reached the northeastern border of Ottawa National Forest. Fred turned down one of the snowmobile paths that cut through it. It was narrow and overgrown, the branches scraping the sides of the truck like the long fingers of an ancient beast.

Fred killed the engine and they climbed out.

They could hear coyotes in the distance.

"Vera!" yelled Moira, cutting the silence like a knife.

Fred followed her call, bellowing with all his might.

There was no response except their voices echoing through the woods, bouncing through the trees in broken harmonies of fearful doubt.

Moira's flashlight caught two pinpricks of light as she scanned the forest.

"What the fuck is that?" Fred asked, freezing midstep.

"I can't tell."

"Get back in the tru-" he had began, but it was   cut off by coarse fearsome grunts.

"GET IN THE TRUCK!" Fred yelled, grabbing her hand and breaking Moira from where she stood frozen in shock, the flashlight falling from her hand and blinking them into darkness as it shattered on the trail.

A gigantic black bear shouldered through the brush that ran along the trail, roaring as it did. Fred could hear its ragged breath as it chased after them. He reached the truck, Moira in tow and shoved her through the open door, climbing in behind her just as the massive beast slammed into the door. He heard the claws scraping at the window.

"Fuck fuck fuck fuck fuck!" He chanted in terrified repetition as he tried desperately to retrieve the keys from the pocket of his jeans.   The bear slammed its enormous paw against the rear driver side window, shattering it into a shower of diamonds which cascaded violently to the floorboard.

He freed the keys and jammed them into the ignition, hearing the bear's claws tearing at the back of his seat, trying to reach him. He cranked the keys and the truck came to life, the headlights reflecting two more sets of eyes in the darkness. Bear cubs.

He nearly put his foot through the floorboard as he pinned the pedal to it, sending dirt and debris flying into the shadows.

One of the cubs ran in front of his truck in an attempt to escape, but instead found only death as the truck connected with it, shattering one of his headlights and breaking the cub's neck. He could have sworn he heard it cry out in one sharp yelp of pain, but frankly he didn't give a fuck in this particular moment and felt the ass end of the truck jump violently as the back wheels crested the dead or dying creature.

The truck flew down the tiny trail, their hearts pumping fear-driven adrenaline.

"Holy shit!" Moira said, laughing in spite of the near death experience, "It almost had you, Fred."

"You're telling me!" he said as he took a hard left, nearly throwing Moira into the passenger window.

"I think we can slow down now, Speed Racer." she said.

He brought the truck to a stop, the engine purring.

"Did you see the size of that damn thing?" he said after several moments.

Moira nodded, "It had to have been three hundred pounds at least!"

"Four hundred," said Fred, sure of his estimate.

There had been bigger ones killed in the Upper Peninsula, but that was the largest he had ever seen in the wild for himself.

"You know what your dad always said, Fred." said Moira through stifled laughter.

"What's that now?"

"If you ever run into a bear in the woods, rub shit in its eyes. If you're worried about where the shit is gonna come from, don't. It'll be there." she had a shit-eating smirk spread across her face that made her look decades younger.

Fred laughed deeply, involuntarily, hunched over the steering wheel. He felt the cool night air creeping in through the shattered window and it felt phenomenal on his sweat covered skin.

"Just for future reference, the .380 is in the back seat." Moira said, still giggling,

"Probably should have mentioned that first, huh?"

Fred frowned at her sarcastically, grabbed the case, loaded the magazine and clipped the holster to his worn leather belt.

"Let's go find our girl." he said when he regained his composure. He threw the truck into drive, "Let's find her."

Chapter Four

Vera moved at breakneck speeds down the trail as she continued her journey eastward. The makeshift crutch had worn a blister under her armpit which finally ruptured. She ignored the pain that invaded her body, knowing that she was so close to salvation.

She had seen the gnarled old oak where the squirrels had been chittering at one another, the ones she had snapped a picture of, and knew that she had found her way back.

Her heart sank when she came upon the campground and found it empty, other campers scared off by the storm or just moving along. Her beloved Jeep was nowhere to be seen. The only sign it had been there was a pile of busted glass underneath where the driver's side window had been.

"NO!" she screamed in fury, collapsing into a pile upon the hardpan parking lot.

She had come this far only to be defeated. Her ankle was now swelled to the size of her thigh and ached deeply in a pain that she once thought impossible. She wept, tears clearing the dirt from her cheeks in small torrents.

She crawled to her tent, the only safety offered to her in the expanse of wilderness that surrounded her. Exhaustion took her before her head could hit the pillow. She woke- covered in sweat- to the cries of the coyotes. She had slept clear through the day. She thought of the ravaged wolf carcass.

"Nasty fucking things." she said to herself.

Her ankle was pulsing with every beat of her heart, and upon checking it found tentacles of red spreading beneath her skin and up her leg.

"No, please, God, no." she cried, tears once again stinging her eyes.

Infection was beginning to set into the wound. Who knows how long that rusted fucking trap sat out in the woods? It looked ancient. It could be tetanus or anything else for all she knew. She couldn't remember if she ever received that vaccine or the booster, if there was one for that.

The gashes from the rusted teeth of the trap oozed a yellowish discharge. She found the first aid kit and bit down on the straps of her pack and poured from the bottle of rubbing alcohol, soaking the wounds thoroughly. The straps muffled her screams but only slightly, and the coyotes answered her with their own howls. She roared back in anger.

She wrapped the wounds tightly in gauze tape, wincing as she did. She chewed four of the aspirin and lay back down, feeling as though she may spontaneously combust from the fever that gripped her. The aspirin was bitter in her mouth and she hated the taste. She felt too weak to retrieve water from the cooler just outside of the tent, but forced herself to do it. She didn't want to risk dehydration on top of the infection and she was sweating bullets enough for it to be a genuine concern.

"Mom, Dad, I love you." she said as she sat alone in the darkness, miles from anyone and further from civilization. The coyotes chuckled amongst themselves and she heard the excited yips. She now knew for sure that this meant that they had found their prey somewhere in the forest.

The pain woke Vera at 3 AM. Stabbing, burning agony that seemed to flow with her blood throughout her body and back down to her ankle in a tidal bore.

She had been dreaming of dead children surrounding her tent, calling the wolves to her. One was Jon, the little boy who had been fishing with his father. He eyes were gone, only black hollows remained, as he stared through the tent flap at her.

The three children from Kitch-iti-kipee howled at the sky, their gray faces stained with blood, joined with another boy, one she had never met, but knew it was meant to be George, the boy who had vanished many years ago beneath the waters of an unnamed stream.

They clawed for her feet through the open tent flap, trying to pull her into the open so that the wolves could feast upon her. The children looked as though they too meant to devour her.

Her fever had temporarily abated from the pills, it would be back soon enough she knew. The chirping of bats was unbearable, there had to be thousands of them out there, gobbling their weight it insects. The crickets didn't help matters either.

Tomorrow she would try to make it back to the main highway. Traffic was sparse, even there, but it exponentially increased her odds of surviving this nightmare. She checked her ankle and saw that some of the swelling had gone down with the weight off of it. The doctors might be able to save it if she could get to them sooner than later.

"God, if you're there, I need you now. If I die out here, I need you to look out for my mom and dad. They've always been big fans of yours, more so than myself." she whispered into the darkness with tears stinging her eyes, "I need you to make them strong enough to handle this. I need to be strong enough to handle this."

She sobbed uncontrollably, "I never meant for this to happen. I'm so lost. If I did something to deserve this, I'm so sorry. If it was the divorce, I understand, but it wasn't all my fault. I tried so hard but he was a monster. He was born broken, or damaged or something. Please just help me, they need me."

She lay thee in the silence as if waiting for a response.

It began to rain.

Moira told Fred to make the next left that came up. They had driven miles on the trails, which had deep ruts and puddles that could swallow cars whole, but found no sign of Vera. They would stop and call for her, being extra cautious since their encounter with the bears, and would hear only the crickets.

Fred made the left, taking them southeast through the wilderness. They could see the clouds beginning to obscure the moon and soon the pitter-patter of rain was hitting their windshield. The drops grew quickly and soon the trail became a muddy obstacle course, constantly threatening to engulf the truck's tires.

"We need to get back to blacktop," Fred said, feeling the ass-end of the truck sliding side to side behind him through the muck.

"She's out here somewhere in this, Fred." Moira said, anxiety palpable in her voice, "Our girl is out here."

Fred nodded but said nothing. They would keep looking, but Fred knew the odds of finding a person in a near million-acre forest was astronomical. They needed help.

The darkness seemed to have amplified a thousand-fold with the disappearance of the moon. and the single headlight wasn't getting the job done to travel faster than forty down even the smoothest of the trails.

"This is all my fault." said Moira breathlessly.

Fred chewed at the inside of his cheek, his own anxiety eating at him, "Don't say that."

"No, you were right about everything." Moira said, grasping his hand. "I'm sorry. For everything, not just this."

"What do you mean?" Fred asked. He knew what she meant.

Moira sighed deeply, "Don't play dumb with me. You know exactly what I mean. At some point I stopped being me and became this...terrible nagging woman."

"I wouldn't say terrible," he said with a risky gamble, "I haven't exactly been the best example of a husband either, babe. I think it's fair to say that we both have made some mistakes."

"Your mistakes didn't cause our daughter to go missing."

"I could have said something to her," said Fred, "I could have told her that you were exaggerating about your trip. I could have said anything."

Moira clearly had not considered this judging from the silence that followed

"You know what I think?" Fred said, "I think that she would have still come here regardless of what we said."

Moira nodded.

"I think that little bastard ex-husband did a number on her, and she was looking for any way to escape it." he finished, his hands tightening around the steering wheel. If Craig had been within a mile of him at the moment he could have killed him dead and felt nothing.

The rain had become a storm and the lightning cast ominous shadows that assaulted their vision with every flash. They heard the rumble of thunder even over the thrum of the engine and wind jostled the trees angrily, blowing the tops in an angry curve.

"I hope she's not out there in this."

The wind threatened to overturn the tent when it raged through like a bull, stronger than it had been with the last front that moved through. The polyester whistled angrily as the wind cut around it. The giant steps of thunder rattled the headache that assaulted Vera- which was likely a result of the crying- and she flinched at every clap.

"When it rains-" she said to herself, but didn't have to finish.

The storm was powerful, she heard several trees crash to the ground under the strength of the wind and hoped that any near her campsite could stand against it. The last thing she needed was a tree crushing her already infected body.

Rain began to pool around the tent, and soon she could see it beginning to slowly seep through the seams above the tarp that comprised the floor of her tent and run down the inside of it in small drips.

"Son of a bitch! Of course, why not?"

She chewed another couple pills, this time gagging at the taste. She pounded back another bottle of water as a chaser.

Lights hit the side of her tent and she thought she could hear the engine of a vehicle over the rain. She scrambled for the zipped flap, her ankle dragging awkwardly behind. The zipper flew up and she spilled out into the deepening water chest first, soaking her shirt. She felt the blister under her arm split as she pushed herself to her knees, crawling toward the lights. It was a truck. A rusty square body Chevrolet.

"Please, help me!" she screamed, "Help me, please god!"

She crawled through the mud, the hidden stones within cutting at her hands and knees like dull knives.

"Thank you! Thank You!" she cried as she drug herself toward the truck. She heard the door open and two sets of footsteps approaching.

She collapsed as they reached her, facedown in the mud. They turned her over and she found herself looking into the face of two men.

One was a face she hadn't seen since her wedding day, Tom Verance, and the other was Craig Daniels. He smiled at her.

"Well, what do we have here?"

Fred and Moira had reached blacktop after nearly getting stuck cresting the hill that lead them to it. He cursed all the way up it, she prayed. The rain relented some, but still beat strongly at the windshield playing an eclectic rhythm.

"Maybe we should go get some sleep and come back out tomorrow with the helicopter?" Moira suggested in exasperation, "This night isn't fit for man or beast."

"Would Vera get some sleep if we were missing?" he asked, raising an eyebrow.

"Probably not." She responded, "I just feel so helpless, Fred. How are we supposed to find her out here?"

"That's the problem with finding yourself," Fred said, "Sometimes you may get lost."

He turned eastward toward the eastern access point of the forest.

"We thought we might find you here." said Tom. He had been Craig's best man on the day they had been married.

"What the fuck are you doing here?" Vera asked, "Please, help me, I'm going to die out here!"

Craig squatted down to look her in the face, "You see, Vera, we took that pretty little Jeep of yours and wrapped that fucker around a tree. You aren't going anywhere."

"It was a sweet little ride, Craig" said Tom, his smile revealing a sparsely toothed mouth, "Too bad that fuckin' turn came out of nowhere. Smashed that sumbitch into the trees."

Craig snorted and spat a wad of mucus into the dirt near Vera. She could smell no alcohol on his breath, which scared her more. That meant he was sober, mean, and coherent.

"Please, I need your help, I won't tell the cops about the Jeep!" she exclaimed, "My ankle is busted and infected! I am going to die if you don't get me to the hospital! Craig, I am going to die!"

They laughed, sending panic into Vera's chest. These men had not come to help her.

"You're right, dear wife," Craig said, laughing, "You *are* going to die out here, because I am going to *fucking* kill you."

She tried to crawl away, but one of them- Tom, she thought- grabbed her by the damaged ankle and pulled her back, scooping mud into her shirt and across her face.

"Where do you think you're going, girly!" laughed Craig, kicking more mud at her, "We're just getting started!"

"Yeah," agreed Tom, "Just getting started!"

Fred saw the sign for the entrance to the forest campground. He stayed here before as a youth with his family on one of his father's weekend getaways, he just hadn't realized until he had seen it.

"Oh, my." said Moira, her hand covering her mouth.

"What?" asked Fred, looking frantically around for something he had missed.

"Nothing it's just… this is where I stayed on my trip. This very spot, all those years ago." she said in quiet disbelief, "It's barely changed."

"Things up here move slower than down home, apparently." said Fred

"Indeed."

The lone headlight led them down the muddy trail towards the camp sites.

"Please, let me go!" screamed Moira, her fingers digging into the soft, wet, earth.

The two men laughed like jackals in the rain, taunting her, "Pleeeeaseeeeee, Pleeeaaaaseeeeee!"

She managed to kick herself free and scurried on her knees toward the tent. If she could only reach the .45 she could end this.

Craig stomped a booted foot onto her broken ankle and twisted.

"You owe me, bitch!" he hissed, "You try to leave me, embarrass me, put me in fucking jail?! It's time for you to get a lesson, Vera. You do not *fuck* with someone's life because you weren't woman enough to satisfy me."

Tom cackled as Craig stomped once again. Vera heard the bones break again and white hot pain assaulted her. She screamed, this time tearing the lining of her throat.

These men were here to take what they wanted and leave her for dead if they didn't kill her. She realized it now. Her saving grace had been a chariot from hell with two demons at the helm and they were doing the devil's bidding.

Vera kicked backward and up with her good foot, catching Tom in the stomach and knocking the wind clean out of him in a harsh, "OOF!"

He gagged and gasped as he dropped to his knees.

"Dumb bitch!" yelled Craig, stomping a third time. "Now you're really gonna get it!"

She pushed the pain away and managed to gain traction, bolting for the tent, running on what was left of her bad leg in a horrific shamble of agony. Tom still lay panting on the ground, unable to regain his breath. Craig tackled her just as she reached the tent and pulled her away from it. He pinned her arms at her side and spat on her before punching her, sending spirals of white flashes across her vision. She threw her hips upward and kneed as hard as she could, sending him over her head face first into the mud.

"Go deep and twist!" said her father's voice in her head.

She felt for the handle of the knife that her father had insisted she take and found it protruding from her boot. She yanked it clear of the sheath and spun around. Craig had just risen to his knees and turned towards her when she swung the blade.

She buried it sideways deep into the side of the man's face where his jaw met his skull. His eyes widened in surprise and the blood quieted his inevitable scream as she twisted the blade. She felt the bones shift and heard an audible crack as his jaw dislocated from its joint. She pulled the knife outward as hard as she could, throwing her weight backward, and felt the knife slide, catch, and then cut through the flesh clear through his face and out of his mouth, blood spilling in torrents into the wet grass.

He grasped frantically at his ruined face, the blood turning his howls into wet gasps of pain. She stabbed him again, this time burying the knife to the hilt in his stomach and then jerked the blade violently. This time the blood could not stifle the scream.

She stabbed him a third time, again burying it to the handle, but this time she planted it in Craig's throat. She felt the blade hit the dirt as it pieced clear through. His eyes widened as he began to drown in his own blood.

"Fuck. You." she said in a growl through teeth gritted so tightly that they risked shattering.

"What the fuck did you do!?" she heard Tom scream in rage.

He had recovered and was standing on his feet in shock at seeing his partner laying in a gutted bloody pile of unintelligible grunts and screams.

Tom shoved his hand into the back of his pants and pulled out a pearl-handled snub-nose revolver pointing it at Vera.

The gunshot rang out, followed by five more. Vera closed her eyes tightly, waiting for the lead to tear her body apart.

"This is how it ends." She thought to herself.

She didn't feel the pain of the bullets tearing through her chest, obliterating her heart and ending her existence. She didn't feel the inertia of the rounds pounding at her chest and she didn't feel her soul leave her body.

She opened her eyes.

Laying face down in the mud where he been preparing to take her life was Tom. His pistol lay several feet in front of him in the muck. Beyond him she saw her father standing, his pistol in hand. Gunsmoke still rolled from the barrel. He approached the man laying in the mud and fired the last round into his head. It jerked violently and sent a spray of red into the grass to be washed away by the rain.

Her mother appeared from behind the men's truck, sobbing as she saw her daughter crippled in the mud, bloody from head to toe.

She remembered her father calling her name as he grasped her in his arms, and then the world went black as she fell into unconsciousness.

The hospital room smelled of cleaning chemicals and the faint scent of vomit. The morphine they administered intravenously brought the dead children into Vera's dreams every night since she arrived three days prior. She couldn't tell if they were real or a hallucination in the state she was in. They would be standing over her bed when she woke in the night, whispering unintelligible words, then they would all throw their heads back in coyote howls until he had to cover her ears to shield them from the shrieks. It did nothing to cessate the volume.

The white hospital blanket was suffocating and she hated the space below her right knee where it lay flat to the bed. It's where the bottom portion of that leg belonged, but it was not in attendance. They had tried to save it from amputation, but the damage had been too great after the mauling it had received and eventually they had removed it.

Craig succeeded in breaking her nose this time around but the fact that he lay dead in a morgue drawer three stories below her current residence was solace enough to make up for that trespass. Tom lay in the drawer next to his. The police pieced together the events of the last week and a half, at least they had made their best guess.

Craig and Tom followed Vera for the entire span of her trip. Craig was stalking her for months, unbeknownst to her and saw her preparations for the journey, then recruited Tom to even the score against her for "ruining his life", as one detective so eloquently put it to Fred, who relayed the message to Vera.

"Looks like they killed two men that were out there cookin' meth." Fred said, his voice seemed distant as though he were speaking through water, "Ditched the Blazer that they stole from downstate and took the dead men's truck. That's what they were driving when we found you."

The two men that Valerie saw in the night watching the tent? The cigarette butts? Had there been a Blazer that had followed her from Kitch-iti-kipee? Had they been there the night that she fled the campground? The gunshots? She couldn't make sense of anything through the morphine haze that hung over her like the rolling black clouds that preceded storms, loud and disorienting to the point of overwhelming terror.

Consciousness was a fleeting concept those first few days; glimpses of conversations, the dead children, the missing leg and the dull pain where it should have been, the sickness from the opiod that pounded through her veins like a stampeding animal with hooves like knives. At times she believed she was dead, her mind floating through the blackness of her subconscious.

It was a week before they lowered the morphine dosage enough for her to regain some semblance of rational thought and another week before they discharged her. The police questioned her about what had happened then and she gave them the details of her journey.

"Did you suspect that your ex-husband was stalking you?"

No.

"Did you do anything to exacerbate his attitude towards you?"

No.

It went on that way for over an hour until Vera finally broke, "I had no idea that Craig had been stalking me or followed me up here! What would you do, *detective,*" she hissed that last part so viciously that the man recoiled, "if you were me? Leg busted to fuck and two men attack you after you crawled miles through the *fucking forest?*"

"Just trying to get the details right, ma'am," he said, his face red with embarrassment.

"The details are that he attacked me with the help of another man!" The outburst had come loud and swift, "I stabbed him in the fucking throat and he's dead. I'm glad he's dead."

She meant it. They thanked her for her time and that was the last she saw of them. There would be no further need for her participation in the investigation, there would be no trial, just two bodies to bury. Vera knew that Craig's parents would likely be on there way to retrieve his body if they hadn't already. She felt pity for them having failed so terribly at being parents. Craig told her of the abuse he received as a child when they first met, maybe that was where the monstrous side slowly emerged from or maybe he was just born that way. Nature versus nurture, the age old question.

Vera felt no thrill as they crossed the Mackinaw Bridge back to the Lower Peninsula. The day was gray and rain slithered down the windows in thick bands, the massive lakes that looked crystalline blue a few days prior now a dull gray of muddied watercolors. Her parents didn't try to stir conversation other than occasionally asking if she was comfortable or if she was hungry. She was neither. The painkillers that the hospital gave her were not as powerful as the morphine and the dull throb of her leg had turned into a sharp one.

She expected questions from her mother and father, and was happy that they had not asked. She couldn't bear the thought of revisiting all that had transpired. She would tell them eventually but not today.

"You ready?" Fred asked, helping Vera into the passenger side of the car.

"I think so," she said, "thanks, Dad." She pecked him on the cheek.

The story made the front page of the Marquette newspapers. Then the Detroit Free Press. Then the nightly news had picked up the story and ran with it. She had been appalled, her life put in the spotlight through suffering. She just wanted to be left alone. But then something changed.

A man named Craig- The good kind- and his son Jon started an online campaign after seeing her to help pay for the mounting bills and prosthetic costs. It had snowballed into an avalanche of donations and well wishes. They surpassed their goal the first week and doubled it two days later. The world had seen her suffering and it offered hope in return.

Her heart fluttered in hummingbird bursts when the prosthesis was slipped over the smooth stump. It conformed perfectly to it.

"Ready?" The doctor asked.

Vera nodded and stood slowly at first, feeling discomfort and soreness and then, after some adjustment by the doctor, it released the pressure and the silicone liner hugged much more comfortably. Her balance felt off, like a child on roller skates. After acclimating to the change she took one small step forward, wobbled, and caught balance. The leg felt bulky and heavy, like sandbags piled on her foot or like an old movie monster goose-stepping after a fallen damsel.

"You'll get used to it," said the doctor, "you'll be a bit wobbly for awhile and it might cause some mild discomfort, but if you really work at it you can do most anything that you want. Airport security will probably be hell though, I've heard."

"It's great!" Vera said and hugged him. The weeks of physical therapy and practicing her balance was paying off as she slowly, yet steadily, walked the length of the room and then returned.   She was overwhelmed to tears.

A year after the first trip- to the very date- Vera returned to Kitch-Iti-Kipee. Marjorie and Chris were there as well. Marjorie had visited her when she returned home and they picked up right where they had left off from meeting. The hour drive from Fenton to Lansing had become a regular road traveled for the both of them.

"Vera!" the kids yelled in unison then mauled her with affection.

"You want a burger or a dog?" Chris asked, "C'mon, don't got all day here, lady."

She flipped him the finger, "Burger, and hold the garlic salt please."

"The nerve of some people, Marjorie!" Chris gasped.

"Shut it, babe." Marjorie said, "Just look pretty and do the cooking." She shot him a wink.

The water seemed much clearer this time, though it had been nearly completely transparent before. She wasn't sure if it was actually was, perhaps it was just an illusion or her own perspective.

Things did seem a lot clearer in general these days. She no longer lived in the shadow of her divorce with the death of her dearly departed ex-husband. There was still time to become a mother too, if re-entering the social world was to go as she planned. She no longer saw the dead children at night, neither did she see the rushing headlights that haunted her dreams, the sound of the truck engine roaring. Her mind was no longer at war with itself, the battle there had been won in gratuitous fashion. She had found peace.

The sky reflected from the water in mirrored beauty that was nearly endless. No ripples crossed the water, the viewing platform now closed for the night. Vera stood quietly at the edge of the oasis, feeling the sun's last rays toast her face warmly. The year had been a difficult, grueling battle, but she was on the downward slope of the mountainous challenges. Life would be different, but life always changes. You just needed adapt to the environment that suits your purpose. In the distance, she heard the coyotes howl.

VERA

Thank you all for purchasing this story. We're sure there are errors that we missed and plotholes that you can find, but we still had fun writing it just the same, we hope you enjoyed reading it.

There is a lot of truth and a lot of false in this story. We won't tell you which is which, decide for yourselves.

Long Live Vera.

Justin And Jennifer Allen.

CPSIA information can be obtained
at www.ICGtesting.com
Printed in the USA
LVHW021651060421
683592LV00009B/847